HOLLYWOOD DREAMING

HOLLYWOOD DREAMING

STORIES, PICTURES, AND POEMS

JAMES FRANCO

INSIGHT EDITIONS

San Rafael, California

CONTENTS

BECOMING
AN INTRODUCTION

I am The Actor.

*

I am The Writer.

*

I am the creator of this book because I am the liver of this life, and at the same time the cut-and-paster of this life.

*

I am a player in the world, and I am an eye on the world.

*

I can make two kinds of movies: one where I go out and fuck with things in the world, where I am the catalyst; and one where I melt into the walls, just an invisible eye, not of the world, only taking it in, where I am in my little hole making sense and order of what I see.

*

Michael Moore in *Roger & Me* or the Maysles brothers on *Salesman*.

*

I am a moviemaker on the page, and I am a poet onscreen. I am a clown performer, *sometimes!* I'm a fun funnyman on Sundays, Mondays, Tuesdays, and Fridays, and oh so serious on Saturdays, Wednesdays, and those black, black Thursdays.

*

When I say I'm a clown, it means that I don't fear embarrassment. That means that my inhibitions are nil; that I know how to take off the restraints and dance; that I can dance, and sing, and write,

and perform in such a way that I can make people laugh. I have the power to make people laugh. Yes, I can make them cry too, but it's the power of laughter that is more valuable.

*

The power to make 'em laugh, it's the best power, you know why? Because laughter is the response I pull out that connects them all to me. When they cries, they does that on the inside, in isolation, in that warm safe place covered in hair. But that laughter, we all hears that, and it connects us—it says, *You is my hyena pack, you is my peoples, my spotted peoples, and we love our spots, we luxuriate in our spots, and we gonna cackle and feed on the corpses of those fallen elephants of culture, those dead corpse monoliths that are still filling this earthbound existence. We feeding and laughing, and the blood is flowing, and that blood flow is art, because we destroyin' but also because we is connected! We communicatin'!*

*

That be the power of laughter, *communication!* An' we all wants that. We in a sea, in a soup—it all mixed up, but if you in the nexus of laughter, you is *never* alone.

*

When I say I have the power to make laughter, it means that I need to be in the right place, at the right time, doing and saying the right things. It be like the magician that needs to be on the right mountaintop, to say the right incantation, in just the right way, and then the lightning will strike his staff, and the people will see, because everything is illuminated. Many of these factors are not up to me, or not *solely* up to me—I need other collaborators. Sometimes these collaborators are other actors, sometimes writers, sometimes directors. And most importantly, the members of the audience are the collaborators, always, because they provide the expectations that I subvert in order to create the laughter. The laughter is the sound of presumptions crashing; the laughter is the noise of me breaking from the mold and going to new places and doing new things. And the laughter is the sound of them coming over to the other side, to the side I'm on, to *my* side, the shadow side, that is sometimes the side of light—the light that shines behind the shapes to make the shadows. Come into my cave; your laughter is the audio that goes with the dance.

*

I'm the scampering squirrel who runs about where the humans can't go, up the telephone pole, into the trees—look at me jump from branch to branch—and I'm cute, and I do funny things with my little hands, and my little mouth. Sometimes I can entertain people just by chewing on a nut.

*

I'm all characters in one: Mickey Mouse (the Leader, the Moral Guide); Minnie Mouse (tha's my sexual, sensitive side); Donald Duck (tha's my angry side, the part of me who gonna fight, but not in a bully way, in a fun/stupid way); Goofy (fo' sure, tha's me, when you're goofy you have bouncy padding all around you, you the foo' and you can do anything, go anywhere, and say anything because yo' goofiness is yo' protection).

*

I don't want to be Lear, I want to be Lear's Fool. Lear has to worry about politics; the Fool gets to say whatever he wants. He's the satellite, the eternal child, the one with all the power because he doesn't need to answer to government, family, love, or criticism; he can just be. He is the

asexual jokester who stirs things up and makes you think about things Oscar Wilde–style, Mark Twain–style, Pancho Sanza–style. He doesn't need answers, he just raises questions—and his lifestyle, the way he be, is the answer. At least the answer for *artists*.

*

I know the Fool in *King Lear* is given his dispensation to be as he is by the authority of Lear, and it is not always easy to be Lear's Fool without Lear, but that's the position you need to find for yourself: Who is your audience? Who is yo' patron?

*

My Lear is God, young women from age fifteen to twenty-nine, stoners, and queers. My Lear is also the Lear I defy—with love. This Lear, this other Lear, is made up of all the conservative fathers and all the prude mothers; he is the wall I bounce myself against called the Main Stream. The Lear I love but lovingly mock is called Pop Culture: I know him well, I am of him, I exist because of him, but I also use him for my work, I use him to make pretty pictures and make pretty rhymes, I pull him in and draw on his face, I dance on his stomach, I pull off his clothes, and I piddle with his dick. I knock him down, *Tiiiiiiiiimber,* and then I play him like a drum. The beats I play on his prostrate body are critical: They are the rhythm that mocks him. They are syncopated rhymes— rhymes that bite, but bite with love.

*

Sometimes when I go to the new places and do the new things—the wizard on the mountain, Moses on the mountain—the new places are in fact old places, and the new things have in fact been done for centuries, and are not so new, but only look new, and I like that, because it means I am linking up with traditions; and I don't mind copying the old because the old is always *new* in a new age. If I put on an old mask, it looks different in the bright electric blaze of today. Before, such a mask was only seen in black and white, and now it's all jazzed up and gay, rainbow colored, just because I put it on in a new age.

*

You see that? It was all about the *choice*, the choice of what to wear, what to like, what to associate with—and the "lighting" of the times will make it look a specific way. That's called context, working the context. Look at how I work the environment—I hardly do anything. I just place myself somewhere and most of the work is done for me. It's an equation:

> **Me** (how people see me; expectations of me) **+ My Performance** (the mask I choose to wear, the part I choose to play) **+ Context** (who is acting with me; who is lighting this shit; who wrote the script; who is directing? Sometimes—usually—all that shit is decided by the collective, by the culture, by the laws and beliefs and ways of life at any one given place and time; as we used to say in high school English class, *"society."* We weren't supposed to use it in our arguments because "society" is unspecific, but we all know about *society*: it be the group pressures, the givens, the tacit understandings about things—what you're reacting against if you're an artist) **= A Work of Art** (an' sometimes life be that work of art).

*

There are many different forms in this book. I would even argue that this isn't a book, it's a movie in words and pictures; an autobiography told as fiction by fictional versions of real people; a collage trying to be a linear reflection of a life that is collage in nature; a clear reflection in a smashed mirror—look at the reflection, but also look at all the pretty cracks!

*

I started many of these stories while I was in graduate writing programs at Brooklyn College and Columbia University, and the poems while I was at the Warren Wilson writing program in Asheville, North Carolina. I did the collages while out in the world, wandering in the world like Satan, working on films: Los Angeles (Chateau Marmont), San Francisco (St. Francis Hotel—*Fatty Arbuckle!*), New York (the Mercer Hotel), London (the Covent Garden Hotel), Montreal (some weird hotel), New Orleans (the W—a disco palace in the middle of the Quarter), Vancouver (the Level—actor haven).

*

When I went to writing school it was a process of *Becoming*. The schools were like factories—I could enter and work hard and come out with a product. The product was my writing, which definitely changed; but *I* also changed. I became something new by working on the new work in the new way. A *Becoming*.

*

The artist makes the work, but the work changes the artist. The parent is forever changed by the child.

*

Because this material was written about a Becoming (the boy becoming an actor) at a period when I was becoming something new (the actor becoming a writer), you can read this Becoming as a paradigm for *all* Becomings.

*

This is not a book, it is a sculpture that you open, like my body and mind were opened—the shell of the actor, the mask of the performer, the outside, which fell aside as the artist bloomed and came out.

*

But when he was born, out from the shell of the boy—smooth in his contours, assured in his approach—he too was wearing a mask. You see, he was just one of a number that live inside me (and you). This be the Russian doll of me. All the layers revolving to the fore, and then being recycled back into the mix to arise again, like a square in the fourth dimension—moving and moving, the inside going outside, and then inside as the writer goes outside, and then inside as the painter goes to the top, and then back as the poet bears himself, etc.

*

A hydra.

*

Because it's about a Becoming, it is primarily set in childhood and young adulthood. This is because the person who is Becoming is always a child, a child growing up; the Very Hungry Caterpillar becoming a beautiful butterfly, young women becoming green witches in the land of Oz. These are the periods of the greatest growth.

*

I wanted to talk about acting and about moving from Palo Alto in Northern California to Los Angeles in Southern California, as a simultaneous ascent and descent. And I wanted to have two distinct periods for the character: 1) his childhood, when he would be called Shrimp; and 2) his young adulthood, when he started acting professionally, when he would be called The Actor.

*

This project ends after The Actor makes it to Hollywood but before he becomes a star. But the stories of Becoming, which end before the full Becoming, are told from the perspective of someone who has become a famous actor.

*

Later I added poems and stories that dealt more with Hollywood on the inside. These are meant to complement the pieces about Becoming. A voice of jaded Experience to go with the voice of hopeful Innocence. But broken, a hazy beacon from the future.

*

This is not meant to be me. Of course there are many aspects of my experiences and many facts of my life embedded in here, but what writer escapes that? What I wanted was to turn everything into something broader, something childish. There are characters with symbolic or unrealistic names, and some of the stories are told as if a child were narrating them, although they are framed in a way that a child probably wouldn't frame them. I wanted to feel the adult sensibility shining through the filter of childhood. The man who has Become looking back on the Becoming, and using the Becoming as the form for the Becoming to be expressed through.

*

As if children and adults alike were being addressed in a children's book; or maybe it's the children within the adults that this child is addressing.

*

There are some devils and some magic in here because this is a world of the imagination. This is where the deadly real world is made sense of through the more powerful, more fun, more beautiful world of art.

THE ACTOR PREPARES

By Shrimp Hello

> NINA: You know, it's quite difficult to be an Actor in your play. There aren't any real people in it.
>
> TREPLEV: Real people! We've got to represent life not how it is, but how it should be, the way it appears to the Dreamer.
>
> —Chekhov

The Actor prepares. He is preparing for a scene. He is backstage at acting class. The acting class is in the Valley, across the hills from Hollywood. It is dark backstage. Onstage, two students mangle the brothers' bedroom scene from *Death of a Salesman*. For some reason they are using Brooklyn accents.

The Actor shuts them out. He closes his eyes and prepares. He concentrates on the misery that he has known. Arrests, breakups, the death of a cat, and the death of his grandfather. Real stuff. Then he imagines fake stuff. His family in a car; they are hit by a Mack truck. Their bodies explode into parts. There are heads on the pavement. Tears form in The Actor's eyes. He opens them. He is in the dark.

His scene partner sits next to him with her eyes closed. The scene partner prepares. She is an earnest, pretty young woman named Ingrid. She has a four-year-old son named Caleb. Ingrid has no husband. Her son, Caleb, usually interrupts The Actor and Ingrid when they rehearse at her house.

The Salesman scene onstage drags on. Backstage, The Actor and his partner are preparing to do a scene from Tennessee Williams's short play *Moony's Kid* Don't Cry. It was written in the dawn of the Glass Menagerie era, right before Tennessee arrived as the new shining light of the Broadway stage. Like Menagerie, it involves Saint Louis, and the working class. Man versus factory. Man The Dreamer, crushed in the machine.

Finally, the Salesman scene ends onstage. Smithson, the teacher, drones. From backstage The Actor can hear him. A low buzz, at a slow pace. The Actor doesn't listen. He knows what Smithson is saying. The Salesman actors are being criticized for their lack of understanding. The Salesman scene is about the conniving vapidity of Happy, and the disillusioned despair of Biff. But instead of those things, the actors were playing two goombahs and missed all the subtlety of the scene.

After five minutes of Smithson's slow buzzing, the wannabe goombahs leave the stage. Two more actors come backstage. The whole acting studio is quiet. Everyone is waiting.

The Actor and his partner go onstage. They do their scene.

The Actor paces around the stage and rants. His character, Moony, works in a factory. Moony rants about his boss at the factory, the Dutch-man. Moony hates the factory. What Moony really wants is to go to the great outdoors and be a lumberjack. He loves the outdoors. Being in the outdoors is the same as being an artist for him. He is dying in the factory where he works.

He dies in the factory because he is ground down by the insensitive machines; Moony's love of the outdoors is a sensitive artist's love for the subtleties of life.

Moony's wife nags. Stop ranting, she says. Don't wake the baby, she says, it will cry. Moony says that his children don't cry. They are tough. Moony is working in the factory to take care of his wife and child. Really, he is trapped by the child, and his sick wife. He calls his wife a sick yellow cat, and strangles her. But then he lets her go. He strangles her because he is trapped; he is just trying to escape his situation. Underneath he is like Blanche DuBois from *A Streetcar Named Desire*: a sensitive soul, trapped and crushed.

Ingrid, The Actor's scene partner, has a real child. Her son is blond like his father. Ingrid has red hair. She has large breasts and a sweet voice, with a little bit of a Czech accent. She and The Actor rehearse their scene from *Moony's Kid* every day. It is usually at Ingrid's house because she has to look after her son, Caleb. Ingrid lives with her parents in Eagle Rock, twenty minutes outside of Hollywood. Sometimes Ingrid's parents look after Caleb when she and The Actor rehearse, but usually her parents have to work. Caleb draws pictures when Ingrid and The Actor rehearse the scene. Sometimes Caleb interrupts them because he wants something to eat; sometimes he wants to show them his drawings. His drawings are of him and his mom and dad, standing on green grass, and there is always a bright yellow sun in a blue sky. His dad is tall in the pictures and has red hair.

Ingrid tells Caleb to draw more. He does.

Sometimes Caleb cries when his mother and The Actor yell in the scene.

Ingrid works really hard at rehearsals, but the scene is difficult for her. She is not really a nagger like the character. She is not a broken, disheveled wife in Saint Louis in the '20s. Ingrid is a pretty, single mother of twenty-five living in LA. Her parents are from the Czech Republic. They speak with accents. They have no religion.

In the scene, Moony has bought a hobbyhorse for his son. A hobbyhorse is like a rocking horse. Moony had one when he was a child. His father bought it for him and they would ride on it together. They would sing the song "Ride a Cock-horse to Danbury Cross" when they rode it. (They also sing that song in the movie Five Easy Pieces, when Jack Nicholson and his friend are cheating on their girlfriends with some women they met at the bowling alley. They all sit around in their underwear, and drink, and sing the Cock-horse song. Nicholson's character's girlfriend, the one he is cheating on, is played by Karen Black. It doesn't make sense that he would be with her because the character is so stupid and cross-eyed, but it's funny.) Moony's father was a drunk who walked out on his wife and child. Moony wants to walk out on his wife and child. Underneath, he is a sensitive artist type. Like Blanche, like Tennessee, like a butterfly. He is being crushed.

Sometimes The Actor and Ingrid rehearse late at night when Caleb is asleep. They have to rehearse the scene quietly so they don't wake Caleb, or

Ingrid's parents. When they rehearse at night, the scene feels more realistic because the scene takes place in the middle of the night. Sometimes The Actor wants to kiss Ingrid, especially late at night, when it's easier to forget who they really are. But then he thinks about fatherless Caleb, and doesn't kiss her.

Their playbooks are blue Dramatist editions. The front cover reads *American Blues: Five Short Plays by Tennessee Williams; Acting Edition.* On The Actor's copy, there is a half-crescent coffee stain and three splotches, like protozoa. There is some doodling too. The Actor has drawn cilia around the protozoa, and crossed out Blues and written pussy. He didn't mean anything by it; he was just bored in class. There are so many words that can go next to *American.*

Vince is in the class. He is a bad actor. But he is slick with women. Smithson, the teacher, is always telling Vince what a bad actor he is.

"Vince, you're such a bad actor," says Smithson.

"Well, thank you," says Vince. "I try."

Vince was one of the actors who did the *Death of a Salesman* scene with a Brooklyn accent. He should have understood the scene better, because in his life, he is like Happy. Vince can get women, just like Happy. He is slick and empty, just like Happy. But Vince doesn't know he is like Happy. Vince thinks he is a great guy who can get women because he is charming and nice. He could have just played himself and he would have been the perfect Happy. But Vince doesn't know who he is.

Vince wanted to be a lawyer when he was younger, but now he's a bartender. He works at the Bel-Air Bay Club on the beach, in the Palisades. Old, rich women like him. He has curly hair, and a nasty smile. The old women like him, but he fucks the young women. After work, at 2 a.m., he takes the young, drunk women out to the beach and lays them down. Sand gets everywhere. Over everything and in everything, butt crack and pussy.

Vince likes The Actor. Vince thinks The Actor is a good actor. Vince wants to do a scene with The Actor. They do a scene from *Beyond the Horizon* by Eugene O'Neill.

Beyond the Horizon is about two brothers, a Dreamer brother and a Farmer brother. It is almost biblical, like Esau and Jacob. The Dreamer brother always looks at the horizon and dreams of being a sailor. The Farmer brother works on the farm all day. The Dreamer plans to go beyond the horizon on a ship to see the world and be artistic. It is like Moony with the great outdoors, a metaphor. Metaphors for being an artist.

The other brother, the Farmer brother, isn't artistic. He wants to stay behind on the farm.

But the Dreamer and the Farmer both love the same Woman. The Woman chooses the Dreamer, not the Farmer. Instead of sailing around the world, the Dreamer stays on the farm to marry the Woman. The Farmer brother takes the Dreamer's place on the ship, and sails away brokenhearted. The brothers have switched places, and then their lives fall apart.

Vince is not a Dreamer, The Actor is a Dreamer. Vince is not a Farmer either, even though he is from Ohio. He is too slick. He is like a lawyer, or an agent. He is bad in the *Beyond the Horizon* scene. Vince is just a bad actor. He should act in *Glengarry Glen Ross*, or be the Gentleman Caller, or play Moe Axelrod. But he is not a good actor, and he wouldn't be able to play those roles, even though he *is* those roles. The Actor is a Dreamer. And he plays the Dreamer in *Beyond the Horizon* well. In *Beyond the Horizon*, he is another Dreamer, like Moony in the other play, whose dreams are ruined by a Woman.

After the scene with Vince doesn't go well, The Actor works on the scene between the Dreamer and his wife. It is from the end of the play, when the Dreamer and the Woman hate each other. The Dreamer has ruined the farm because he is a Dreamer and not a Farmer. He is now sick and dying, but his wife still hates him. His brother, the Farmer, has traveled, and seen the world in the Dreamer's place. The Farmer doesn't appreciate seeing the world, or sailing (the metaphor for art). He is just a Farmer at heart (a businessman).

When The Actor and Ingrid rehearse the Dreamer/Woman scene from *Beyond the Horizon*, they rehearse late sometimes.

Back in class, while Smithson lectures, The Actor quietly tells Vince that he wants to fuck Ingrid. The Actor is worried about Ingrid's vagina because she is a mother. Vince tells The Actor that it will be fine. They are whispering because they don't want Smithson to catch them.

"It will be fine," Vince whispers. "Don't worry about that baby, that shit is like elastic, closes up. You won't fall in."

The Actor is afraid he will fall in.

(The Actor had sex with a Czech girl once. It was in Prague. He was visiting. Someone took him to a brothel called K-1. He went into the room and had sex with a young girl. She was actually not Czech. She was Russian. A Russian prostitute. But she was very thin and not very pretty. Not as pretty as Ingrid.)

The Actor and Ingrid rehearse late many times, but The Actor doesn't kiss Ingrid. The scene from *Beyond the Horizon* isn't romantic. It is too hard to find the moment to kiss Ingrid because their characters hate each other.

One night, at 1 a.m., Caleb wakes up and comes into Ingrid's room while The Actor and Ingrid are rehearsing. Caleb is crying. He has had a nightmare.

Later, The Actor is backstage at acting class. Ingrid is there too, in the dark. The Actor prepares. It is hard to prepare. He has had a good life. Except for a few DUIs, he can't think of any painful memories. The power of his grandfather's death has faded. He feels nothing for his dead cat.

He needs to feel bad for the scene. He uses his imagination. He thinks of little Caleb standing in the road. Caleb gets hit by a car. His head comes off. The little head with blond hair rests on the pavement. The Actor cries.

Ingrid and The Actor do the scene in front of the class.

The scene takes place eight years after the Farmer brother has left on the boat. The Farmer is expected to return to the farm that day. He is a rich man now. The Dreamer is a failure. The farm is falling apart because the Dreamer couldn't take care of it.

The Dreamer is sick and dying, but he is in denial. He says that he just has *pleurisy*, but really, his lungs are about to give out on him. He has consumption or something like that, a disease from the old days. The Actor plays the denial and sickness well. He coughs a lot and stumbles around the stage: a man trying to act healthy who is about to die. The Dreamer still has dreams of doing something artistic with his life. He says that he and the Woman will move to the city so he can be a writer, but it will never happen. He will die soon.

The Dreamer suspects the Woman of really loving his brother, the Farmer. The Dreamer thinks that his wife is excited for the Farmer's return, because she is really in love with the Farmer, and married the wrong brother.

In the scene, The Actor and Ingrid have to use stage whispers because the Woman's mother is sleeping in the other room.

The Dreamer and the Woman also had a child, but it died.

After the scene, Smithson tells them that they were great. Smithson says The Actor is indeed a sensitive artist, and he knows how to play the part of the Dreamer very well. Smithson tells them to do a scene from *The Seagull*. Smithson normally doesn't let people do Chekhov, because it is too difficult for LA actors, but Smithson thinks that they can do it. It is a big compliment.

The Actor and Ingrid rehearse *The Seagull*. It is not a romantic scene, but Treplev loves Nina so much that it is pretty romantic. The Actor acts as if he loves Ingrid, for the scene. In his real life, The Actor thinks about Ingrid as if she were Nina from *The Seagull*. He thinks about how much he loves her.

One night, when they are rehearsing, they do the scene and something happens. The scene begins:

NINA: There is someone here.
TREPLEV: No one is here.
NINA: Lock the door, someone might come.
TREPLEV: No one will come in.
NINA: I know your mother is here. Lock the door.

The characters are alone. Treplev has had his heart broken because Nina fell in love with another man. She fell in love with a vacuous writer named Trigorin. Trigorin and Nina had a child together, but it died. Nina and Treplev talk in the scene. Treplev tells her how much he has cursed her, and hated her, because she ran away with the other writer, Trigorin. Treplev the artistic writer makes fun of Trigorin the vacuous writer. Treplev says that Trigorin thinks he is Hamlet, but really, Treplev is Hamlet. Treplev quotes the line from *Hamlet* that everyone quotes, because it is the easiest to remember:
"Words, words, words."
In the scene, Nina keeps saying that she is a Seagull. Earlier in the play, Treplev has shot a Seagull. (Just like Mariner shot the Albatross in *The Rime of the Ancient Mariner*.) Nina is like the Seagull, destroyed. She has been destroyed by the vacuous womanizer, Trigorin.
Treplev wants Nina to stay. He still loves her. He is lost as a writer. He can't find his way. But she doesn't stay, she leaves. She is an actress now.
At the end of the play, Treplev shoots himself, offstage.

One night, Ingrid and The Actor are rehearsing the scene from *The Seagull*. They meet very late. When the characters lock the door, Ingrid and The Actor really lock the door to Ingrid's bedroom. When Treplev says that he has kissed the ground that Nina walks on, and has been warmed by the memory of her smile, The Actor says it, and really means it. The Actor has been warmed by the memory of Ingrid's smile, all those times he thought of her as Nina. The Actor kisses Ingrid. She is surprised. She is still in the scene. The Actor keeps kissing Ingrid on the mouth. Then Ingrid is not Nina anymore, she is Ingrid. Ingrid wants to kiss. She kisses back. She has been so lonely; she wants this kiss. They kiss. The Mother and The Actor. They fall onto Ingrid's bed, and kiss. They take their clothes off.

Outside the door, Caleb is knocking. He has had another nightmare. He tries to open his mother's door, but it is locked.

Later, The Actor and Vince are backstage in the dark. They are at the acting studio, of course. They are preparing for a different scene. It is a scene from *True West*, where one brother is a writer, and the other brother bullies him into writing a bad screenplay. The Actor plays The Writer, Vince plays the Bully.

In the dark, The Actor whispers to Vince. The Actor is excited; he tells Vince that he slept with Ingrid. Then Vince whispers,

"Yeah, me too."

The Actor is quiet. They can hardly see each other's faces in the dark.

They both sit there, backstage, in the dark. The scene *on*stage is from *A Streetcar Named Desire*. It sounds bad. Stanley Kowalski sounds like a twelve-year-old girl. Ingrid is in the scene onstage, playing Blanche, but she is not very good either. She is not a good actress unless she is acting with The Actor.

"Was it good?" whispers Vince.

The Actor doesn't say anything.

"I told you you wouldn't fall in, right?"

Silence.

"Matronly tits, right?"

The Actor prepares. He sits in the dark. His eyes are open. Even though his eyes are open, he sees Ingrid on her bed, naked. He sees himself and Ingrid kissing, like they did. Now the kissing has a sour taste. Vegetable green and rotten.

Vince and The Actor do the scene:

For once, Vince is good. He bullies the fuck out of The Writer/Actor. There is something of his Ohio backwoods roots that comes out. Vince is frightening, imbecilic, and dangerous. He threatens The Writer with a golf club; he even brings it down on the table, hard. (A big no-no at the acting school.) Vince stomps around the stage and barks about the Western he wants to write. He is passionate. He *really* wants The Writer to write that bad Western. The way he says it, it's as if *Vince* really wants the bad Western to be written.

The Actor acts poorly. He just sits next to the prop typewriter and mumbles his lines.

After the scene, Smithson talks. His voice is low and slow:

"Good, Vince, good. That is the best scene you have ever done. But Don't Damage Our Furniture."

"Sorry," says Vince.

"That was the most real acting you've done here, Vince," says Smithson. Vince looks happy. "You really understood that part. I don't know what it was, but you got it."

"Thank you, sir," says Vince.

The Actor sits sullenly on stage. He is still next to the prop typewriter, and the battered table. He doesn't look into the audience. He doesn't want to see Ingrid.

Smithson addresses The Actor:

"And that was your *worst* scene."

The Actor looks at the floor.

"I don't know what to say, except that you were *not* in it. You need to be listening to your partner, reacting to him. You were just sitting there in your own world."

The Actor prepares.

At the beginning of *Moony's Kid Don't Cry*, it doesn't actually specify that the scene takes place in Saint Louis. When The Actor did the scene, he just assumed that it took place in Saint Louis because that is where Tennessee Williams lived when he was younger. The Actor was projecting Tennessee's life onto the play. What the stage directions in the play actually say is:

SCENE: Kitchen of a cheap three-room flat in the industrial section of a large American city.

The scene is not specifically in Saint Louis. It could take place in any city in America. Just a Dreamer, a Lover, a Child, and a Villain. It could happen to anyone.

PART I
POEMS

SPRANG BRAKE

YOUNG BITCHES

When I think of them bitches, young and curvy,
Young stars in an age of Internet legends,
I think about how they is, and they isn't, they own.
When you're young, and you a star, your body

And yourself is the objects of the ruling class,
And that ruling class is the entertainment class.
Harmony, that enfant terrible, plucked these eager
Things from their *Teen Vogue* nests and put them,

Like pink gems, in the crown of his rude empire,
So they could be paraded around like the baubles
They are. But also gave them a little respect.
You see, they were eager, so eager to get inside

The game of authenticity, because they lived in the land
Of candy, but what they didn't know was that their value
Was their gingerbread forms, their sweet sugar bodies,
And these were the things that Director puppeted about.

LIKE A MUG SHOT

My life is like a mug shot, a portrait taken
For a crime, because you see, we is only
On this earth for a short, short while,
So why we gotta do all this frettin' fo' nuttin?

So that crime I speak of, it's the way I go
In the face of all that's considered decent,
Because what they consider indecent is the takin',
And what I consider worth takin' is them little

Thangs all wrapped up in them bikinis like bows,
On presents waiting in Florida-Christmas colors.
You see, this place is hot all year round, like hell,
And I be the Debil rulin' the roost, *Satan* Claus,

With dem ho, ho, hoes. But they all got them mug shot
Faces too, because they come from the world where
Decency is doin' what Mommy says, except they got
Them bodies that done got them all in twouble.

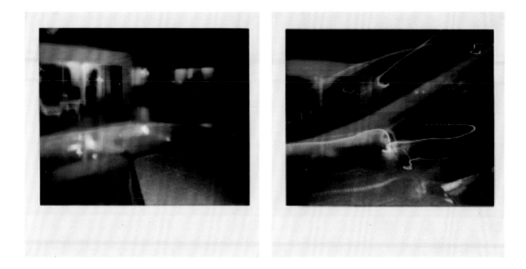

NEON

E'eryone who ain't from Florida
Think that neon is the most,
Most important thing about it,
An' they right. They is right.

That bright colored light
Is all they iz, that's all we iz
Doin' on this planet, ain't we?
Making pretty pictures

For each other to tantalize
And dominate each other
For sex, power, and reproduction.
That light encapsulates all

Of this, a fiery center
Of dangerous pink, zinc
Blue, humming chalk
White, vibrant lemon.

HAPPY

Happy day, bitch; look at this mutha-
Fucka, look at this kiiing. Do yo' thing.
I'm down for this, I'm down for all.
It's like when you're playin' that game

And the screen starts to ripple, water-
Like, and you enter into that world
And you're *in* the game? That's it,
That's what I've sworn my life to.

I'm *this* dude, this one you're looking at,
With the tattoos on his chest
And the grillz in his mouth
And the cornrows planted down his head.

I'm the gangster of these virtual parts
And you might say that this simulacrum
Ain't real, but that's like saying a karate
Master on a mountain, lost in Japan,

Is more powerful than *The Karate Kid.*

DOPE BOYZ

In the film I play a rapper slash gangster,
I'm a G to the end—that's a G for *gangster*—
But it's also a whole lifestyle. There's this guy
Named Riff Raff, who claims I used him.

He's this jokester-style mutha-funker
Who raps. He started his shit on MTV
With *G's to Gents,* one of their silly shows
That use youthful ignorance and dumbshits

As comedic fodder. Well, this foo' ain't bad
In his clownish way, he's a good rhymer
And appropriator of culture, all shit I love.
But for this character, I did some other kind

Of work, I done followed a real gangster
Named Dangeruss, a man with dreads
Like a lion, who lived the life on the streets
That he sings about, the real deal, the scary.

And he's in the film, representing, representing.

COOL HOUSE / REAL HOUSE

Welcome to the century of crime, bitch.
Welcome to the world where crime
Is entertainment. Welcome to the world
Where the specter of apocalypse

Rears its head with global warming's
Fiery menace, when there is no safety
Even in yo' own trap because we all
Is watched, and drones is alive.

Where you gonna go to find something real?
To get to the true you need to use the fibers
That make up the world about us:
Bricolage, a system within systems

That allows us to engage with the world
About us, even as it consumes us.
Paris Hilton becomes art, like Britney Spears
Becomes art, like Mickey Mouse becomes art,

Like computers become art, become human.

ANGELZ

That was a time we had down in F-L-A.
It was something, like with all movies,
That was special, like a bubble, in which
We all lived, a magic time, where we all

Came together. This is how it iz on all filmz
But this one was special, because them girlz
Was doin' sumptin like this fo' the first time
And they wanted to be rescued, di'n' they.

At first they was excited, and said yes, yes,
Then they was scared, and pulled back,
Because they waz still loyal to all them fanz
Of theirs, the young wunz, impressionable.

But then it changed, once again, when I arrived
Because I waz the electricity that shocked dem
Into place, you see how that happened?
They was hot young things with skillz of sex

That I brought to the fore, and galvanized.

MAKE MONEY

They ain't much to life, is dey?
Iss a doge-eat-cat world an' I'm
A tigress, *la tigra*, *el lyon*, Egypt-
Born prince, a sphinxy pharaoh,

And I spread around seven plagues
Like I was god against them others.
I'm tha chozen one, Mexican Messiah,
Cool Hand Luke, and Han Solo.

I eats my steaks with my heart,
And my eggs with my legs,
And I'm running marathons for long
Hauls, like I'm training for something:

Armageddon. Miles of money,
It keeps piling up like I caught something.
The money bug, I'm sick with money, I'm
Aladdin's Genii, I'm grantin' myself wishes,

Muhammad Ali Baba, boom baba, boom.

MASK

When I wear this mask,
It's a little bit of inspiration;
I'm a ghost in a zombie nation,
So I can walk through and steal

Like the wraith we've all become;
Ain't no individuality, ain't nun,
When everyone is walking round
With a gun; so fuck it, cops

Is killers, and video games is fun,
And there ain't no diff'rence
Between grand theft auto
And *Grand Theft Auto*, nun.

I'm living in a video game,
Living in *Vice City*, an' this mask,
It ain't a mask, it's a badge,
I'm the El Capitán of this gang;

It's a flag, I'm a nation, bang.

Hellish

CARTER / FRANCO

Cleaning the teeth with friends.

Blue flowers, shaving, the face.

Reading. ~~A good~~ book
Hellish Animal.

An Intruder's hand.

Awakened by Spirits

A VISITOR.

Resting...
...It was all a dream.

Together.

Celebration.

Bored. Deacadence.

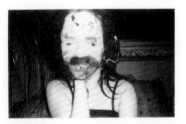

Trying things.
Ghostly.

Waiting. Waiting. ~~Unnnnnn~~

~~Many~~ ~~matar;~~ ~~although~~ Like
They Enter (but it seems ~~although~~
They were always THERE)

It all unfolds.

The Ghost. The man. The shadow.

An Arm, a Couch, a Carpet
The Room is Quiet Again

Hovering Above.

Chased through Sculptures.

Faster!

Hellish Animal.

Everywhere.

... And Many.

If we hide, They won't find us.
I know This to be true.

I will hide too

"Remember who you Are."

Lost in Mirrors.

Down. Down.

an Apparition. A portrait.

In between.

CAUGHT.

She was beautiful,
and died.

aid placed, ~~aptetra lite~~

Carried from Danger.

Within, Through, although.

Safe.

Joe Wilson

The Weight of...
Thomas Janes

Harvey Milk

What Just Happened
Sean Penn

Friends
Eric

Willie Stark

The Interpreter
Tobin Keller

Samuel J. Bicke

Paul Rivers

Jimmy Markum

Loved
Man on the Hill

I Am Sam
Sam Dawson

Cuco Sanchez

Rowley Flint

Emmet Ray

Strange Hitchhiker

1st Sgt. Edward Welsh

Hurlyburly
Eddie

Conrad Van Orton

U Turn
Bobby Cooper

David Kleinfeld

Eddie Quinn

State of Grace
Terry Noonan

We're No Angels

Judgment in Berlin
Guenther X

Colors

Daulton Lee

Henry 'Hopper' Nash

Crackers
Dillard

Mick O'Brien

Buddy

Jeff Spicoli

Taps
Cadet Captain Alex Dwyer

The Killing of a Randy...
Don Fremont

Hellinger's Law TV mov...
Bit Part

Barnaby ... TV series
Sam

... the Prai...

SEAN PENN

A PLACE
IN THE SUN

ELIZABETH
TAYLOR

MONTGOMERY
CLIFT

SEAN

A PLACE IN THE SUN I

His leather jacket kicks it off so well,
Under the opening credits—printed large—
As he hitchhikes on the side of the road;
An indelible image that was Kerouac,

Jack London, Tom Cruise, Matt Dillon,
And my acting infancy.
Now I watched the film with a part-Irish,
Part-Cherokee beauty, with a cheekbone face

And a long elfin body to match, slung
In a cherry-red G-string and nothing else, bundled
In a cloud of Chateau sheets. She remarking
On the close-up beauty of young society Liz;

I silently noting the deft reticence of Clift when caught
In the woods: the leather, now with a Hawaiian shirt.

A PLACE IN THE SUN II

If each of the three had two movies that hold performances
As defined and remarkable as God and Adam
On the Sistine ceiling, they would be *East of Eden* and *Rebel*
For Dean; *Streetcar* and *Waterfront* for Brando;

And fucking Monty's would be *From Here to Eternity*
And *A Place in the Sun*. There is something so perfect
About the likeable murderer he crafted with George Stevens
In noirish black and white. A frightening,

Striking attack on romance and finance from Dreiser.
Dreiser, Dreiser, Theodore Dreiser,
An abridged version of Dreiser, ready to kill
With brevity and succinct plot accumulation.

He was just a young man on the rise; can't blame the boy
For such a situation. I can understand.

A PLACE IN THE SUN III

Three perfect performances: a young man
Swirling in his back-lot room, with *Vickers*
Flashing in neon out the window: his mind exposed;
A young woman/angel, the actual Vickers,

An apparition too good to be fucked—
You can't blame the hero for sinking ship,
And jumping ship, when one ship was loaded
With *baby on board*; and the Shelley Winters

One, *mamma mia*, what a performance.
To play such a sniveling wet rag
With no holding back; I'm in love.
Goes to show you, there is no hope

For the ugly. All we want is Monty and Liz
To love and love and love. But Shelley, *I* love you.

A PLACE IN THE SUN IV

When Dean played in Stevens's *Giant* he was hoping
For the intimate portrait Monty gave
In *A Place in the Sun*, but instead got a man who shot
And shot and shot, from every angle; *the around*

The clock method, Dean called it. He was in Marfa hell.
But Monty got to play in the intimate world
Of Stevens, where a subtle half grin or a blank stare
Registered like revelations.

There is a little room for coincidence. Randomly,
He runs into Shelley Winters in the movie theater;
But all of that is just leading us to the situation
We need for tragedy: a tough dilemma, with no easy way

Out. There are beautiful settings and shots, but they are all strung
On the taut line of dramatic tension.

A PLACE IN THE SUN V

When asked, I should say that *A Place
In the Sun* is my favorite film,
But I rarely do, I guess because I forget
How effective the black and white

And the wide shots that let the action play;
And the very selective use of close-ups,
Saved primarily for hazy, angelic filter shots
Of Angela Vickers—that's Elizabeth Taylor—

Beauty shots that establish her as the young man's
Objex of desire, establish his subjective lust.
Not even Monty gets a close-up in some of these scenes.
Also, one close-up toward the end, the scene

When Monty's caught, there's a strange old man waiting in the woods.
The shot feels most real of all: his scruffy face releasing cigarette smoke.

A PLACE IN THE SUN VI

In the paradisal bed—with the sheets
And the girl in the candy-red string panties—
I was haunted by the parallels
Between Monty's situation as George Eastman,

And Monty's situation as Monty and myself.
(I love my life.) But George wanted to rise: have money and have the girl.
He convinced himself that he could love Shelley Winters before he knew
He could have Elizabeth Taylor. I know I've done the same,

Except I don't try for the Liz Taylors anymore; if they come, they come;
But that's how you do it, just share the bed with any old body,
And most times they'll be nice ones—especially if you're a movie star.
(I like how Liz comforted Monty in the film like she did in life.)

And don't think love won't exist: "I love you. I've loved you since the first
Moment I saw you. I guess maybe I've even loved you before I saw you."

ELIZABETH TAYLOR

Grand dame, gorgon Martha
Versus your silver tongued beau
Sir Richard as George.
That was the *later* you,

The you who passed through Cleo-
Patra, and brought down a studio;
The you who was James Dean's
Shoulder to cry on in *Giant*;

The young you who played Monty's lover
In *A Place in the Sun*, and his heart's support
In life. Could you comfort him
After his crash in the Hollywood Hills,

When his face was readjusted
And he became frail and busted?
You climbed into the accordioned wreck
And pulled teeth from his throat.

Poor Monty, he became a shadow,
A slouched figure in too-big pants.
You got big and drunk and weird,
You went on *General Hospital*.

Every once in a while they would drag you out
To give an award and you'd slobber on the mic.
But you were all those things from before
And all those versions of you, frozen on celluloid,

Especially in long lens close-up,
Opposite Monty, at the dance,
So young and natural,
And that look right at the camera;

"I love . . . [*gasp*] are they watching us?"

MONTGOMERY CLIFT

Before Brando and Dean.
A new American way of
Fucking with the camera.

Your soul fluttered
Behind your stone-still face,
A Donatello statue emanating
Deep life on the flickering film.

Burly Burt Lancaster feared you
Because of your latent power;
You played your character in
From Here to Eternity like a human

Knife in a Hawaiian shirt.
In *A Place in the Sun*, the longing
And sorrow and sociopathic
Intensity vibrate through

Your handsome mask.
Like nothing before or since—
A minimalist artwork,
Motionless as it clobbers.

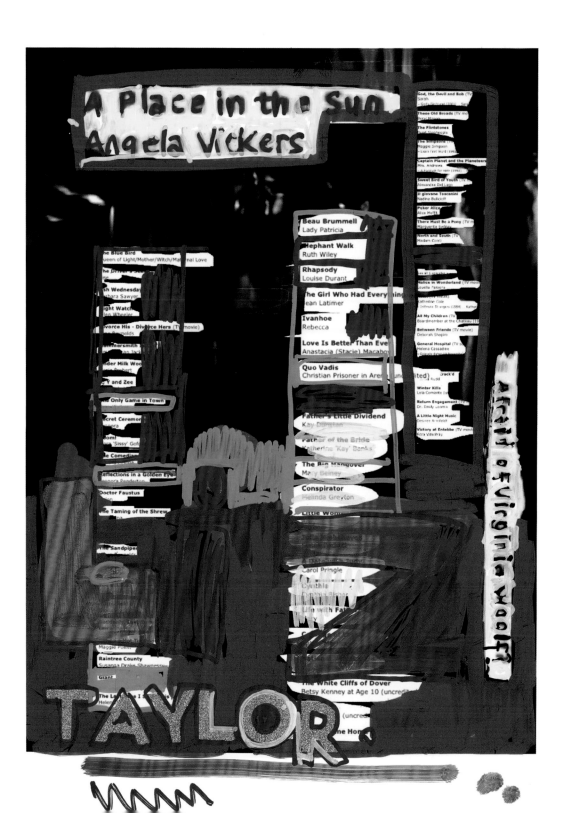

SEAN I

Sean was a son of a Leo,
An actor himself,
Who filled in for Gazzara in
Cat on a Hot Tin Roof
And played in *The Girl on the Via Flaminia*.
Blacklisted by Odets, in the age of blacklists,
He came back as a television director.

You, long-haired teenager in Malibu,
A gang of you: Sheens and Penns and
Lowes,
By the pool and big dreams.
Father Sheen: *Apocalypse Now*.
Brother Penn with his 8 millimeter.

You sons of actors,
You pack of brats,
You lover of Madonna,
You fighter of paps,
Big drinker,
Coke sniffer.

No wonder
You befriended Brando,

You made Jack Nicholson a pal.
No wonder you needed to direct,
To get political, to live
A life of meaning once again.

But you can act, we all know.
When you played evil in *Mystic,*
And when you played gay in *Milk,*
That was as good as it gets.
You might never get better.

Except for that narration
On *Dogtown and Z-Boys*:
Talking about the old days
Of surfing and skateboarding
And your hometown, Malibu,
Before everyone got old,
Got arrested, or died.
You use the older man's gruff voice
For the news of the boy you were.

That was the truth.

SEAN II

They called you Sean
De Niro because of your
Dedication. An actor
As engrossed in his role
As De Niro, as LaMotta,
You were Spicoli, stoner,
Prophet, entertainer, politico.

Smart enough to know
Not to give too much:
That ordering pizza
In class was the move
That would last.
Everyone loves a loser
If he smiles; everyone
Wants to relax.

Spicoli, in his dream, won
Surf contests, and had babes
On his arms, and was asked:

"A lot of people expected
Maybe Mark 'Cutback' Davis
Or Bob 'Jungle Death' Gerrard
Would take the honors
This year." You said,
"Those dudes are fags."

And when he introduced you
For your nomination for *Milk*,
De Niro, now your friend, said
He couldn't believe you
Had been cast in all those
Straight roles, because
In *Milk* you were such
A fine homo. And when
You and I kissed
On Castro Street, it was for a full minute.
Your beard was like my father's.

SEAN III

When New Orleans drowned
You pulled out a shotgun,
Got a boat, and rowed
People to safety. When
Haiti fell you went
And did things
On CNN.

At the hotel you did coke
Off the web of your hand,
At the *Vanity Fair* party,
Crazy eyes,
You pinched it
And sniffed.

Help, help, help.

In *The Beaver Trilogy*,
A little-known thing
You did before *Fast Times*,
You played a cross-
Dressing Olivia Newton-
John impersonator who
Got his makeup done
At the morgue.

SEAN IV

In *Taps* you were tough
But straight-laced;
Tom Cruise was the crazy.

At Close Range:
There is a legend that
To get a reaction
Out of Chris Walken
You said to the prop man
So that Chris could
Overhear, "Fuck this shit,
Put in the real bullets."

In *Bad Boys*
You played a bad boy
Of the dated '80s.
In *The Falcon and the Snowman*
You changed your voice
To high and nasal.
In *Casualties of War* you played
A wartime rapist, and in
Shanghai Surprise

You worked with your wife,
The first wife, and boy
Was it bad.
But you know.

The Indian Runner,
The Crossing Guard,
The Pledge,
Into the Wild: wild
Rants about inner
Torture and fighting
For a way out. You
Wanted a way out,
A way out of the actor.

You were an angry young man
And you're an angry old man.

There is no home left,
It changed while you raged in Haiti.
There is no home anymore,
Please come home.

69

PART II
SHRIMP STORIES

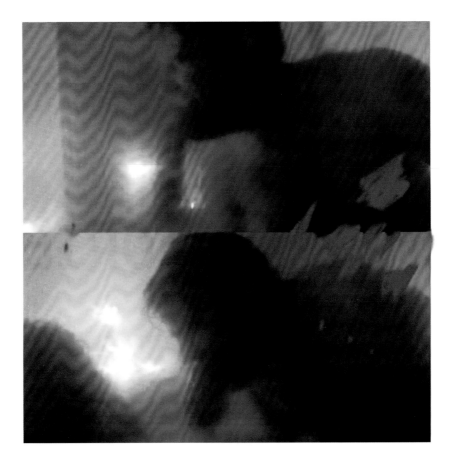

VAMPIRE

MR. AND MRS. HELLO

This is a story about the Hellos. It's a story, but I tried to make it real. Here's the beginning:

Mr. and Mrs. Hello lived on Emerson Street—named after that famous thinker/writer—in Palo Alto, California. The house was small, white, and boxy and sat at the end of a quiet cul-de-sac. The cul-de-sac was cut off by a cement-covered creek, called Matadero. There is little to say about the Hellos now. They are a very quiet couple. Of all the quiet couples in all of quiet Palo Alto, they are probably the most quiet. But they were not always that way.

They had wild times in the '60s at Stanford University. Stanford is right next door to Palo Alto. Back then, Palo Alto wasn't so boring, and neither were the Hellos. There were tons of drugs and the Hellos did plenty of them. The Grateful Dead grew up in Palo Alto; they were called the Warlocks back then, and they came back to play often. Ken Kesey was in the area, doing stuff. He had gone to Stanford for the Steigner program and had worked at the VA hospital in Menlo Park when he wrote Cuckoo's Nest. During college, the Hellos had a place in La Honda, a forest community to the west of Palo Alto, where the Kesey Acid Tests originated. That was a pretty important place to be. Neal Cassady and Allen Ginsberg were about. And the Hells Angels.

Sometimes, Mr. Hello, when he was old and spiritual, would tell stories about their crazy neighbors in La Honda.

"The landlord had told our neighbors to leave because they wouldn't pay rent. These people were crazy, and so the next day they left a dog's head on the landlord's doorstep. There was no way to prove that it was them, but everyone knew."

"Was it the landlord's dog?" asked Shrimp. Shrimp was their son, kind of.

"No, the landlord didn't have a dog. It was just a random dog."

"What kind of dog?"

"I don't know, a freakin' black Lab or something. I didn't see it. They probably bought it at a pet store and killed it."

"What did they do with the rest of it, the dog body?"

"I don't know. Fuck, Shrimp." Mr. Hello swore sometimes, even though he was spiritual now. "Fucking buried it or something. Cooked it, maybe." He looked down at the meal he was eating, greasy chicken, and said, "Probably tasted something like this."

"Shut up, Guy," said Margot Hello. Mrs. Hello liked to call Mr. Hello Guy, even though his name was Eugene. She liked saying Guy.

"So, anyway, the landlord was still making them leave, even after the dog," said Mr. Hello. He was picking at the chicken that Mrs. Hello had prepared. Shrimp ate as little of his chicken as he could, pulling the gray-and-pink meat from the bone with his teeth and then dropping it onto his plate. "So they left a piece of dynamite on his porch with an alarm clock taped to it."

"Did it blow up?"

"No, Shrimp. It was just a threat, like they were saying they would have blown him up if he made them leave. But they didn't. They left and nothing happened."

"Oh."

"Then one time I found a bucket of blood on the road. Just a bucket of blood."

"What do you mean?"

"There was a bucket full of blood out on the mountain road."

"What did you do with it?"

"Nothing. I just saw it."

Shrimp was twelve. He liked to write stories. He wrote this story you're reading. (Hi!) He was the Hellos' son, but not really. He was different from them, but he liked to hear old stories. There was also a son named Shark.

He didn't like word stories; he liked TV. He was the Hellos' real son, and he fit with them best. Shrimp was curious and artistic; Shark was loud and aggressive. Shrimp was fascinated with Ken Kesey, and Neal Cassady, and the Hells Angels. He asked the Hellos about them. Everyone was in the living room doing different things:

"Did you meet Raymond Carver?" (Because Carver had lived in Palo Alto when he met Gordon Lish—people Shrimp didn't know about then, but who he would learn about later. I'm just making him more precocious than he maybe was.)

"I know someone who knew him, Raymond Carver. His name's Andy. My friend's name," said Mr. Hello.

"What was Ray like?"

"I dunno."

"Shut up, Shrimp! I'm watching *Growing Pains*," said Shark.

The Hellos didn't know much about that good, writer stuff; they were just around when all the stuff happened.

"Tell me about the murder in the Stanford church," said Shrimp. It was a true story.

Mr. Hello looked at him gravely. Mr. Hello and Shrimp were sitting on the couch. Mr. Hello was working on a complicated math problem while Shark watched TV from the easy chair, and Mrs. Hello, in her own chair, was sewing the new cat's name onto a Christmas stocking. Below the name (which was Lincoln) was a decal of a little gray mouse with a little white tail that she had sewn onto the stocking already. The Hellos all had stockings, so the new cat needed one too. Shrimp's stocking said Shrimp, and had a little gingerbread man on it.

Math problems were Mr. Hello's hobby. As he worked at the long, snaking equations that drifted down the pages of graph paper, one to another, like numerically constituted dragons, Shrimp continued with his pestering questions about the Memorial Church murder.

"It happened back in the '60s," said Mr. Hello. "She was a young woman, new to town. She was walking home one night. She went into the big Memorial Church. Mrs. Stanford built that church for her husband,

Leland Stanford, after he died. In the morning, they found the young woman raped with two candles inside her, and an ice pick in her head. There was semen on a prayer pillow next to her."

"Guy, don't tell him that," said Mrs. Hello.

"Did they ever find the killer?" asked Shrimp.

"They never found the killer," said Mr. Hello. "They say it was the Son of Sam."

"Who is Sam?"

"No, the Son of Sam."

"Who is his son?"

"No one—I mean, he was the killer. David Berkowitz. Sam was a dog that talked to him."

"A talking dog was Sam? Wow."

"Something like that, but I think that's all made up anyway."

"What, the talking dog?"

"Yeah, and that the Son of Sam was alone."

"Alone in the church with the lady?"

"Hungh— oh, no. I mean when he did all the other killings. It was probably a cult."

"A cult killed the woman in the church?"

"It wasn't the Son of Sam," said Mrs. Hello without looking up.

"Or maybe it was Ted Bundy," said Mr. Hello. "Or the second Manson."

"No," said Mrs. Hello. "No, it wasn't."

"Who, then?" asked Shrimp.

"Shut up!" said Shark. "I'm watching." Shark never wanted to hear the stories. He only liked to watch television. *Roseanne* and *Growing Pains*.

"The candles were inside her?" asked Shrimp, quieter.

"Yup—two of 'em," whispered Mr. Hello.

"He made her eat the candles?"

"No. They went in a different way."

The Hellos knew a few weird stories, but for the most part the Hellos lived quiet lives. Mr. Hello was in telecommunications.

"What is that?" asked Shrimp, one Saturday after his soccer game. Mr. Hello was driving him home. Mr. Hello came to the games to watch. Shrimp wasn't very good, but he tried.

"I just work with numbers, and do codes, and organizing," said Mr. Hello.

Mr. Hello hated his job. Back in his Stanford days, he had wanted to be a poet, and after that, he had wanted to be a painter.

"You did?"

"Yup."

"Why did you stop writing poetry?"

"I don't know. I just did," said Mr. Hello. "Well, I wanted a specific professor. This great poetry professor named Yvor Winters—he's why I went to Stanford in the first place." Mr. Hello was driving and drinking a latte from a large Styrofoam cup. There was cinnamon powder on the top of the foam.

"Can I have a sip?"

"Yeah, but be careful." The foam was good, and the cinnamon was good, but the coffee was hot, strong, and bitter. Shrimp gave it back.

"Ivor, like Igor?"

"No, Yvor with a Y. He was a very famous poet, but more famous as a teacher. He had been friends with another famous poet named Hart Crane before Hart jumped off a boat and killed himself in the 1930s."

"Why'd he do that?"

"Hmmm. Lots of reasons. I guess because his dad didn't support him even though his dad was a millionaire. His dad sold chocolate, and even created Life Savers—you know, the candy shaped like a lifesaver from a boat. But he sold the patent to that before he could make any money on it. And Hart was an alcoholic; and he was gay but never really found anyone to love in his life, and even slept with a woman right before he died; and mostly because he wrote poetry that was very difficult, that no one liked, and even his friends like Yvor said it was bad."

"You were in college in the 1930s?"

"Hungh? No, Hart was, and Yvor. Yvor was a very old man when I went to Stanford in the '60s. That's why he stopped. The year I went there was the year he stopped teaching."

"You wanted him even though he said bad things about Hart?"

"Hungh? Oh, it didn't matter. He was still a good teacher. And he probably felt bad about what he said later, especially because Hart became a much more important poet than Yvor. Robert Lowell, John Berryman, Allen Ginsberg, and Tennessee Williams all loved Hart Crane—or maybe they liked the figure of the man more than his work."

"What do you mean?"

"They liked that he was gay and tough and suicidal as much as they actually liked his poetry."

"His dad liked that he was gay?"

"What? No, his dad didn't know he was gay—Hart kept it a secret because his dad would have hated him even more than he already did."

"You would hate me like Yvor if I was gay?"

"What? No. I will always love you."

"You didn't have Igor?"

"Yvor, no, he was gone, I think because he died, so I started painting. That's how I met Mom."

"What kind of painting did you guys do?"

"I don't know. A little abstract. I painted women's legs."

"Why?"

"I don't know. Mom painted brides, but the veils would mix with the faces and they always looked like grated cheese."

The first time the Hellos met, a little scene:

Eugene Hello is twenty. He has long hair like a hippy. He's wearing a button-down denim shirt. He's handsome. Margot Vice's hair is down to her butt. She's pretty, albeit short. She is not yet "Mrs. Hello."

In class, Eugene Hello walks over to Margot.

"I like that one," says Eugene. He points at one of Margot's bride paintings.

"Thank you," says Margot.

Eugene looks at all her paintings. They are all laid out. All brides.

"You like marriage."

"No," she says. "These are sad brides."

"I like your stuff," he says. "It has a groovy naiveté." It is a compliment the way he says it.

"Oh," says Margot. "That's what Richard said." Richard is their teacher.

"Oh. Well, he's right."

After that, they painted together, sometimes all night. Margot and Eugene. They went to parties together. Sixties hippy parties.

One night Margot does LSD. She thinks: If the record stops spinning, I will die. She doesn't die. After two months, Eugene and Margot move in together. They rent a place in the hills of La Honda. They have crazy neighbors.

They go to more '60s parties. Margot never does drugs after the record night, but Eugene does everything. He does lots of cocaine.

One day Eugene's father calls. He never calls. He is an old bearded World War II veteran of Portuguese extraction. He is a principal at an elementary school. He is an alcoholic. He says, "Stop painting at Stanford, or I won't pay. Do something else."

Eugene is mad. He hates his dad. But after that, Eugene Hello stops painting and goes into mathematics. He does lots more cocaine. Eugene Hello never speaks to his father again. Eugene Hello and Margot Vice finish at Stanford, then Eugene marries Margot, and then she becomes Mrs. Hello.

Back to now:

In the hall closet, behind Mrs. Hello's unused cleaning supplies, there is a cardboard photo album with a large brown stain on the front. Sometimes Shrimp looks at it. It has the photos from the Hellos' wedding. It was at the house of Margot's parents, the Vices, in Shaker Heights, Ohio. Eugene Hello is twenty-one years old in the pictures. He smiles at the camera. His eyelids are half-closed, and his green eyes are milky. His hippy hair is gone, but his bangs are long in the front and hang just above his eyes. He looks like a poet, but he isn't. Not anymore. This is the moment before he left for business school, and stopped being an artist.

Scene from the wedding:

    After the ceremony, there is a reception at the Vices' house. Eugene Hello goes out to the garage with his friend, God.

    "Eugene, what the fuck are you going to do with your life?" says God. God is a painter.

    "I'm doing lots," says Eugene Hello.

    Eugene and God do coke in the Vices' garage. Margot Vice's sister, Sunbeam, is with them. Everyone else is back in the house. After the coke, Mr. Hello goes back inside the house. God stays in the garage and fucks Sunbeam.

In the pictures of the wedding, Mr. Hello slouches on the oak banisters of the old house, and on the shoulder of his wife. They are now Mr. and Mrs. Hello. Mr. Hello looks evil. He has very long teeth, like an eel. They're yellow and sophisticated teeth, resembling the teeth of an old English duke. He's like a fucked-up British eel on the shoulder of his little wife. The British side is from his mother. His Portuguese dad is not in the pictures. Mrs. Hello looks scared. Oh look, there are God and Sunbeam in the background. Sunbeam looks like she has been fixing a carburetor in the garage.

Some more stuff:

    Mr. Hello got into business school at Harvard, and Mrs. Hello moved to Cambridge, Massachusetts, with him. The winters were cold. The days were boring. Mrs. Hello stopped painting all the time. She'd only paint a little, at night. In the day she taught elementary school while Mr. Hello took classes. One day, after teaching, Mrs. Hello was walking across the Anderson Memorial Bridge on campus as a team of rowers was just about to pass under it. They were rowing in unison and seemed unified with the river, their reflections moving in sync beneath them, embedding them in the sun-clapped surface of the water, and then in turn the river felt unified with all the trees along the bank and, beyond them, the old edifices of Harvard. She didn't like rowing, or Cambridge, but she thought, That is a magic moment, and she wanted to keep it.

Later she learned that the Anderson bridge was where young Quentin from The Sound and the Fury leapt to his death. It was strange because the bridge was not very high. It was almost as if Faulkner had written about a place he had never been to.

At home, Mrs. Hello looked at all her paintings. All the brides. They didn't capture any magic like the magic of the moment when she had seen the rowers. Those bodies rowing in unison.

"These brides look like grated cheese," she said to herself. She threw them out. She never painted again.

Then all she had was the teaching. She taught first grade one year and then kindergarten one year. She wanted to communicate with these children, to tell them about the world, to let them know that all was not perfect in the world, but they would survive if they knew how to depend on themselves. She also wanted to let them know that all the feelings they had inside, even the bad ones, were okay and natural. She started writing children's books to communicate these ideas to her students. They were part fairy tales, part real world. Little stories about a boy who lived in the normal world but had special powers, powers he didn't ask for but that he had to deal with. In the stories they were magic powers, but she wanted those powers to stand in for intelligence, talent, and good looks. She didn't know who the boy was; he was just born in her work. Maybe it was her future son.

When the Hellos moved back to Palo Alto, they were still in their twenties. They moved back because the happiness they had found while painting together had left when they were in Cambridge, but they had been happy in Palo Alto before, and they wanted to find that happiness again. They had been married three years, but there were no kids yet. They hardly had sex. Mr. Hello did too many drugs.

"Why did you guys come back to Palo Alto?" asked Shrimp.

"Because I finished business school and we liked it here. And I got a job," said Mr. Hello.

"Where? Doing what?"

"What is this, an interview?"

"Yes."

Mr. Hello got a job at a company called RAKEM in Silicon Valley. He hated the job, but he saw it as a temporary situation. When he got out of RAKEM, after he'd made enough money to support a family, he was going to contribute something significant to the world. What the contribution would be took different forms in his daydreams. He would discover a mathematical formula that would be named after him. Hello's Law of Fractions. Or he would get back into art. Maybe sculpture this time. Tiny bronzed legs of women.

He worked at RAKEM and the cocaine was still going, but pills were better. They kept him speeding all night. Eventually he stopped doing much of the telecommunication work he was hired for and just played computer games. This was in the old days in the seventies, so the video games were just little shapes, circles, and squares for Paddle-Ball, and just words for this one called Colossal Cave Adventure where you would walk through magic caves and there were evil dwarves. That was a great one to think about because you couldn't see anything—all the images were in your imagination, like (later) when you read about the hobbit, and the dwarves in the goblin caves: You read about them and came up with all the images yourself.

After a while of the too much drugs and the games late into the night, Mr. Hello was let go from RAKEM. Now peek at the Hellos from this time:

Mrs. Hello is thin with mousy brown hair. She scuttles about on little legs and stays at the house all day. She has an artist's heart and is terrible at housework. Fly carcasses collect in the screens of the windows around the house. Mrs. Hello is a terrible cook.

One night she cooks a pale and bloody chicken. It looks blue in places because it hasn't been cooked enough. It is coated in slime. She brings it to the table.

"That looks like an abortion," says Mr. Hello. He isn't hungry. He just wants to do drugs.

The next night Mrs. Hello tries again. She makes quiche. It is black on top, and in the middle, it has the consistency of brain.

"I feel like I'm eating a fucking brain," says Mr. Hello. He goes out to the garage and does drugs.

After that day, Mrs. Hello stopped cooking and spent all of her time writing her books for children. She had written every day since that moment on the Anderson bridge. And she wasn't teaching anymore, only writing. It was as if her writing were her teaching, even though no one read her stuff. She thought that someday they would. Her ambitions were humble:

"I just want to write a book for children. Something that children will like. I can do that," she would say to herself.

She was not happy with Mr. Hello, but she wrote her stories and she felt okay. She wrote about a little boy who was a wizard. Here is a little bit:

> Teddy was not like other boys. He was the chosen
> one. He had a mark like Cain on his forehead
> that set him apart from the others, even the other
> wizards. He was the best boy there was. He could
> do magic at a very young age and he was very brave.
> The way he got his scar is very mysterious. An evil
> magician named Satan came when he was a baby
> and tried to kill him. But Satan could not kill him.
> He only scarred him.
> It was an indescribable mark. Often people would
> remark about the mark, but after Teddy was gone
> they would say, "That mark was indescribable. I can't
> describe it." But if you think about it, even though

Teddy was so good, he was such a good, special boy, he was also marked by Satan. And that is no little thing.

Mrs. Hello didn't get anything published, but she kept writing. She had a little office at the back of the house. It looked onto the backyard. She could watch the red-breasted robins while she wrote. They pulled worms out of the ground like rubber bands, and ate them. The office was her special place. She cleaned the fly carcasses out of the screens of the office windows, but none of the other windows in the rest of the house.

Mr. Hello went to Silicon Valley every day to work at ROLM, a new place that had hired him, and then came home and sat in the garage and did his drugs. He had learned enough from working at RAKEM to try to do his drugs at home. He liked the garage for doing drugs. There were no cars in the garage; it was for storage only. But there was an autumn-colored couch that was turning green from the dampness. In the dark, he would smoke filterless Camels and listen to music on his big headphones and do the powders and pills. The drugs felt good. Lots of beer, too. Whole garbage bags full of Coors that Mrs. Hello carried to the curb each week. She would do it at the last minute, right as the garbagemen arrived, so that the neighbors wouldn't see the bags. All the garbagemen got to know her.

Mr. Hello never slept. Except at work sometimes—but very carefully, so that he wouldn't get caught. He looked like a ghoul. His green eyes had turned gray.

One night Mrs. Hello came out to the garage.

Mr. Hello looked up. His eyes were squinty black lines. The music was loud in his headphones.

"I'm going to Cleveland," said Mrs. Hello.

Mr. Hello took his headphones off, the music still audible yet muffled: Mick Jagger.

"Don't give me any shit," said Mr. Hello. He didn't know what she had said, but he knew she was on his case. "You're no better than I am," he said. "Just a little wife."

"I *am* better. I don't do drugs. And I'm tired of all this drinking."

"Bullshit. You do as much as I do," he said.

Mrs. Hello thought this was pretty funny. Especially because her husband was serious. She hadn't done drugs since the LSD at Stanford. Mrs. Hello would have laughed if she didn't have an embryo in her uterus.

"You're not the man I married," she said. "Or maybe you are and I didn't realize."

"You and your little books. Fuck you, fuck you, fuck you. You know, when I met you, everyone said you were the worst painter in the class. Richard said your paintings had a naive charm. Well, they were naive shit."

Mrs. Hello cried a little. She wasn't surprised, because she cried a lot now. Then she stopped. She wasn't doing this for herself. She was a mother now. She had to be responsible.

"Well, Richard was a better lover than you," she said, and left. She knew it was a stupid thing to say, and it wasn't true, not really.

A year later, they had a fat little son named Shark, and a steady lifestyle. If they didn't look too hard, the Hellos had everything they wanted. Mrs. Hello could write in the mornings before spending the day with Shark. Mr. Hello had stopped doing drugs, so Mrs. Hello had stayed with him. Mr. Hello went to work and came home for dinner most nights. But he still drank his beer and occasionally he got drunk and yelled at Mrs. Hello and sometimes at Shark.

"You fucked Richard, hungh, you fucked the great teacher? Dick, Dick, Dick, the great Dick teacher! Well, what the fuck is that bum doing now? A fucking *artist*, hungh. A fucking *bum*."

"I don't know," she would say as she pulled Shark from his high chair.

"Probably *his* fucking kid," said Mr. Hello. "He's not my kid, that little Shark."

But that kind of outburst was rare. Mostly their lives were routine. Mrs. Hello had her writing, and Mr. Hello had his computer games and dreams of the art he would do one day to get him through the long days at work.

A year after that Shrimp would arrive and then it would be Shark and Shrimp. The Hellos were not perfect but they were doing their best in a crazy world where computers were taking over.

The sight t[...]

ROLM/ZOO

It was a gray Tuesday. The sky was filled with thick clouds; they looked heavy and about ready to explode. At 8:00, Mr. Eugene Hello got ready for work. He put on a boring gray suit while he listened to Bach. He liked Bach. He had been off drugs for a year and classical music helped him. He also liked looking at trees. He was thirty-one. The Hellos lived on Emerson Street in Palo Alto. It was a cul-de-sac. Mrs. Margot Hello had been up for three hours writing her book. It had been coming along very well that morning. Some very scary things were happening to the boy in the book. A demon was trying to kill him, and there was a giant snake.

When Mrs. Hello heard her son, Shark, crying, she went into the nursery and nursed him. Shark was one.

Outside, there was a howling noise. It was very distant, but it sounded like the howling of people being burned in a fire. But the Hellos didn't notice. Only the cat, Lincoln, noticed. He was black and white, and his markings made it look like he had a beard and a top hat. When Lincoln heard the howling, he ran down the hall and skidded across the floor on his nails into the living room. He gathered himself and stuck his ass in the air; all his hair was on end. He hissed at nothing in the corner where the Hellos put the Christmas tree in winter. No one noticed.

At 8:30, Mr. Hello took his brown coffee mug, black coffee inside, picked up his office papers, and went to kiss Mrs. Hello goodbye. In the nursery, Mrs. Hello's tit was hanging out, and Shark was crying. Mr. Hello kissed Mrs. Hello on the forehead. Shark was screaming, so Mr. Hello didn't kiss him.

Outside, the air was cold and Mr. Hello heard a high-pitched whistle. It was faint but constant. Mr. Hello wandered down the walkway, past Mrs.

Hello's white Subaru wagon, and got into his charcoal-gray Honda Accord. He turned on Mozart and backed out of the driveway, looking over his shoulder with his hand on the back of the passenger seat.

At the end of the block, he started to feel dizzy.

"Are you dizzy?" a lady asked.

"Yes," he said to no one. No one was in the car with him.

"Hello?" he said aloud. "Is there a lady in here?" No one responded. He said to himself, "No, there's no lady, but there is a fucking idiot in here."

Then he suddenly kicked at the brakes. The car jerked two times and then stopped. There was a wolf in the middle of the street. A gray, haggard wolf. Its head was slung low, and there was ropy drool falling from its mouth onto the road. The wolf stared at Mr. Hello. It had yellow eyes, tilted into sinister diamonds. Mr. Hello sat there and looked at the wolf. Then he thought about his wife and child being eaten by the wolf. He pressed the gas hard with his heel and tried to run the animal down, but it slipped out of the way. It trotted onto the sidewalk and into the backyard of Shirley, the neighborhood piano teacher.

Shirley Nichols was a man. Music arose from his house every evening because of the piano lessons he taught. Mr. Hello had tried to talk to Shirley about Mozart and Bach at the block party last summer, but Shirley had said, "Let's not discuss the masters over hot dogs. Let's give it a rest, shall we?" *Give it a rest? Fuck you, you old swish fuck.*

Mr. Hello said a silent prayer that the wolf would eat Shirley, and he drove off.

Mr. Hello sat in traffic on Oregon Expressway. He thought about some numbers and programs for work. Especially the numbers 3, 7, and 9, and a certain program. He was in telecommunications. It was very boring, but he was trying his best to be a good employee now that he was off drugs. Sitting in traffic, he also thought about his little son and his wife. He saw them sitting in the house, the image of them when he'd left them, his wife's tit sagging a little.

Then he saw a weird thing. Ten gray wolves were running between the stopped cars. They had hunched shoulders and dashed along in quick bouncing steps. Their mouths were open and it looked like they were smiling. Mr. Hello looked to the car next to him to see if anyone else noticed the wolves. There was a woman with a brunette bob and a heavy jaw. She looked like an eggplant. She was staring off at the gray sky. Probably contemplating suicide.

Mr. Hello looked back and the wolves were gone. He looked in the rearview and saw nothing; he looked back over his shoulder, but there were no wolves. The traffic began moving.

Mr. Hello's office was a low white cement building. It was called ROLM. It was pretty much the same as his old job at RAKEM, but at ROLM he didn't do drugs. He was clean now, no more drugs. Mr. Hello always sat with his back to the window in his office. There was usually nothing interesting outside his window. A gray wall, a few gray pipes, and a little bit of gray sky.

That morning, while he was working on the program he had been thinking about earlier, out of the corner of his eye, he thought he saw something large flying across the patch of visible sky. When he turned to look, there was nothing. He faced the window for the rest of the morning, but still there was nothing. The sun was hidden behind gray clouds. Far off, on the vast underbelly of unbroken cloud, there was a black stain.

At lunch, Mr. Hello decided to get a burrito from the food truck that regularly parked on the street.

He left the white building and walked along the gray path that cut through the lawn. As he walked, he did not think about much. He had forgotten about the wolves. He was very hungry. A burrito sounded good. He smiled a little.

Gray clouds pressed down on the earth. They were pregnant and writhing. There was no one around.

Then he saw The Devil. The Devil was standing at the food truck drinking black coffee and smoking a cigarette. Mr. Hello tried to be cool as he walked past The Devil, but he couldn't help looking at him from the corner of his eye. The Devil just stood there leaning against the truck and smoking. Mr. Hello ordered his burrito. Steak with cheese and guacamole. Rick started making his burrito. Mr. Hello knew Rick from the burrito truck (he made good burritos). But he also knew him from the drug meetings he went to. Mr. Hello was off the drugs but still struggling with the drinking, and Rick knew this.

Rick didn't notice The Devil, and Mr. Hello didn't want to point him out to Rick while The Devil was standing there. There was no one else around except The Devil. Mr. Hello looked at The Devil.

"Hello," said The Devil.

"Are you real?"

"Yes, I'm real. Mr. Hello, right? You have a little son named Shark."

"What do you know about Shark?"

"Nothing. I don't give a shit about Shark. I just don't want him to be lonely."

"He's not lonely. He's fucking fine. Leave him alone."

The Devil flicked his cigarette butt and walked off.

"Don't touch Shark, you devil fuck," Mr. Hello yelled at The Devil's red back. But then The Devil was gone.

"Your burrito is ready," said Rick.

"Did you see The Devil, Rick?"

"I didn't *do* nothing," said Rick.

"I know you didn't *do* anything. I mean, did you . . . no, never mind."

Mr. Hello stood at the cart and took a few bites of the burrito. He looked around for people, but no one was around. He ate alone. The chunks of meat were hard and dry and caught in his throat because he didn't chew properly. Mr. Hello thought of chicken farms and slaughterhouses—long rows of cages, and feathered animals covered in their own feces, and cow carcasses lying on the ground. He forced another bite. There was a small gumlike piece he couldn't chew. He squeezed it between his molars, but it wouldn't break apart. He spit the piece onto the top of the burrito and threw it all into a trash can. There was no bag in the can. The metal container clanged.

He heard someone say, "Moron." He looked around, but there was no one. Rick was gone, too, somewhere in the back of the truck.

Mr. Hello hurried back to the office. He called his home, but Mrs. Hello didn't answer. He tried two more times. Then he sat and stroked his beardless chin. *I just saw The Devil*, he thought. *Devils don't exist*. He got back to work.

It was very difficult to concentrate on numbers after that. They got jumbled in his mind, and he added things incorrectly. He was also very hungry because he hadn't finished his burrito. He finally left the building at 5:00.

He wasn't feeling well. He had to take his coat off while driving because he was sweating so much. His face was hot, but the sweat was cold. The chilled drops rolled down and stung his eyes with their salt. His shirt was sticking to him under his armpits. The sun was partially visible, dropping into a pumpkin blaze against the grape clouds.

Thirty minutes later, he pulled into the driveway of his home. Mrs. Hello's white Subaru was in the driveway. He parked next to it. Then he saw the wolf. It slipped into some ivy at the end of the street. Beyond the ivy, there was a cement creek, but his view of it was obstructed. The wolf was in there.

Mr. Hello got out of his car and started yelling. He was yelling at the wolf, even though he couldn't see it.

"Get the fuck out of here," he said to the ivy. "Get the fuck out of here, you Shirley wolf fuck."

He could see someone looking at him from the side of a curtain in the house next door to his. The Bacon house. Mr. Bacon was an astronaut. He had been on the moon twice. The curtain slipped back into place. Mr. Hello stopped yelling at the wolf and collected himself. He had been yelling pretty loudly. He took his office papers from the car. He was embarrassed.

At least the Bacons had a bad son. Ollie. Ollie Bacon was twenty-three and still lived at home. He was always being arrested for drunk driving and stealing. It made Mr. Hello feel better to think about the Bacons' bad son.

He decided not to tell Mrs. Hello about the wolves or The Devil.

"Hello, honey," said Mr. Hello. He was acting normal. He put his papers on the counter very casually and kissed his wife on the cheek, like he hadn't met any Devils that day.

"How was your day?" he asked.

"My day was normal and nice," she said.

At dinner, Mrs. Hello told Mr. Hello some gossip about the Bacons' son. Today she'd learned that he'd gotten a teenage girl pregnant. Mrs. Hello had been in the backyard watering the orange tree when she heard Mrs. Bacon talking on her phone.

"She was crying about it. I felt so bad. I wanted to help her."

"You can't help them," said Mr. Hello. "People who go to the moon don't need our help."

"It sounds like the girl's parents are pressing charges," said Mrs. Hello. "She is only seventeen."

Mr. Hello wasn't listening. He was thinking about The Devil. He tried to eat the chicken that Mrs. Hello had made. It was undercooked and covered in clear, greasy slime that made a ring around his mouth whenever he took a bite of his drumstick. He had agreed not to criticize if she started cooking again. He looked at his son. Shark was eating some apple mush.

When Shark was in bed, Mr. Hello went into the living room and turned on the TV. He watched *Full House*, but he wasn't really watching. He was in another world.

Mr. Hello sat very still. He felt cold and alone. Mrs. Hello came into the living room and sat on the couch with him. She was a small woman. Her legs didn't touch the floor. She moved closer to him so that their thighs were touching. She watched the show. A cool girl was pressuring Stephanie Tanner to smoke in the girls' room.

"Do you think Shark is lonely?" asked Mr. Hello. He was still staring at the TV.

Mrs. Hello looked at him.

"No. He's just a baby. I spend all day with him."

Mr. Hello didn't say anything else. Soon after, they went to bed. Mr. Hello couldn't sleep. He was sweating. In the middle of the night, Mr. Hello got up and walked back to the living room and looked out the window. He didn't see any wolves. He went back to bed.

In the morning, Mr. Hello dressed and kissed his wife goodbye. He even kissed Shark, although Shark was screaming very loudly. Mr. Hello was determined to have a good day. When he stepped out the front door, he almost stepped on the baby in a basket resting on the front porch.

There was nothing else in the basket—just a baby wrapped in a blanket. It was sleeping.

Mr. Hello called in to work and told them that he would be late. Because he had been doing so well lately, it was not a problem. Mr. Hello, Mrs. Hello, and Shark all drove to the Stanford hospital in Mrs. Hello's Subaru: Mr. Hello concentrated on driving, Shark was in his car seat, and Mrs. Hello held the baby.

There were no identification records at the hospital, and when the police were called they had nothing they could do immediately, and since there was nothing else to do, the Hellos decided to keep the baby until he was claimed. They left a contact number and took Shark and the baby home. Mr. Hello went to work, but he couldn't focus. He didn't even eat lunch. He stayed in his office and thought about The Devil.

Saturday morning, the hospital called. After a three-day search, the baby's parents could not be found. If the Hellos didn't take the child, it would be sent to a foster home.

They called him Shrimp.

He was The Devil's son.

Because the Hellos didn't know how old Shrimp really was, they said he was Shark's age. They celebrated his birthday on the day they found him, that gray Wednesday in November. The 4th. Time passed.

Nothing ever happened in Palo Alto. The sun rose and the sun set. Shark and Shrimp were regular boys. When they were seven, they would kill bugs with a magnifying glass. The bugs would smoke and die. Sometimes Shark pulled the legs off the little frogs he found in the backyard. Shrimp told him to stop, but he wouldn't. Sometimes he would only pull off one leg so they jumped lopsided. Shrimp would find them and try to be nice to them.

Once he ate one of the frogs. Just a little one, and he was already missing his legs from Shark. Shrimp just swallowed him so that he could live in Shrimp's belly.

Sometimes Mr. Hello would play Nintendo with Shark and Shrimp. He loved *The Legend of Zelda*. There were so many puzzles to figure out, and figuring out puzzles was something that pleased Mr. Hello. Life was a puzzle, but it was nice to have a puzzle that was solvable every once in a while.

Over the years they forgot that Shrimp was a foundling. But strange things often happened around Shrimp, and they'd be subtly reminded that he was a little different. Once Shrimp got lice and Mrs. Hello shaved off his hair. The next morning all of Lincoln the cat's hair was shaved off too. They locked Shrimp in his room for a week.

Another time, Shrimp went to the bathroom. After, when he was about to wipe, his shit flew out of the toilet. It smeared itself all over the walls. It even started writing words on the wall. On the mirror it wrote, *I hATE the HELLos AND FAT FUCKr shARK*. He was grounded for two months.

But, for the most part, Shrimp seemed like a normal kid. It was only in hindsight that his actions, the actions of any young boy, seemed to carry special significance. And, heck, just the fact that his actions were *looked* at in hindsight gave them more import than they'd had when they happened. The looking made them seem like the actions of a Devil child.

Then it was Shark's tenth birthday. Shark's birthday was in the middle of the summer.

The morning of Shark's birthday, Shrimp woke up from a bad dream. In the dream, he was carrying a black cloth bag and a man was trying to stick it with a knife. The man kept laughing and stabbing with his knife.

When Shrimp opened his eyes, he saw a daddy longlegs on the ceiling. It was doing its slow, delicate walk across the crease where the ceiling, met the wall.

Shrimp lay looking for a minute, then rolled to the side and put his feet on the floor. He stood and put his clothes on. Shrimp was small and skinny. He had brown hair and brown eyes. He had buckteeth and a scar on his forehead. He was told that he'd gotten the scar from falling when he was a baby.

He went into the kitchen. He took down the box of Lucky Charms from the cabinet and poured the colorful shapes into a white bowl. He also poured some into a bowl for Shark, because it was his birthday.

The Hellos were going to the zoo for Shark's birthday. Shrimp was a little scared. He hoped nothing happened while he was there. But he was also very excited to go to the zoo.

Mr. Hello drove. Nobody spoke. They listened to Bach. Listening to the music, Shrimp could see gray armies crashing together in slow motion, and an old man in an old, red drawing room, looking very serious and staring.

"I had a dream about a demon," said Shrimp. "He was trying to stab me."

"No demon talk," said Mr. Hello.

It was a sunny Saturday and the zoo was crowded. Mostly families. The Hellos went in. They started with the monkeys. The gorillas had their own island with a house and ropes hanging from the trees. If a gorilla punched you, you would die.

There was a baboon behind glass. It had a long red-and-blue nose and yellow eyes. When Shrimp stood in front of the glass, the baboon ran at him. It pressed its hands against the glass and shrieked at Shrimp.

Next, they saw spider monkeys. They were tiny and black, with skinny legs and arms, and funny tails that they could hang from. They had their own little mountain to climb around on. They looked like they were having a good time. One was on top of another one. The one on the bottom was a woman spider monkey, but it was hard to tell because she looked like the boy spider monkeys. People laughed when the boy monkey kept jumping on her back. She would keep pushing him off. They were fucking.

At all the cages, there was a big sign that said *Don't Feed the Animals*.

At the chimpanzee cage, there was a man throwing pieces of his hot dog and hot dog bun into the cage. The Hellos stood back and watched. The man wore a flower shirt and a floppy tan baseball cap. He was surrounded by a bunch of people who were laughing. He didn't have any kids with him. When the man threw, the chimps would race to the pieces of hot dog and put them in their mouths very fast. They would push each other, and screech, and then wait for the next piece. Then, the man threw a big piece of hot dog at the chimps and it fell into the moat. The chimps really started screeching. One of the chimps picked up some of his poo and threw it toward the man. The poo went really fast and splattered some of the people around the man. Everyone was screaming and laughing. The Hellos and everyone except the man backed away from the cage. The chimp and the man kept throwing poo and hot dog at each other until some people from the zoo came and yelled at the man.

The Hellos went to the Lion House.

The building was made of stone. There was a sign that said *Whole Rabbits Will Be Offered at Today's Big Cat Feeding*. Inside the Lion House, it was loud and crowded. There were animal sounds and lots of people talking. It all echoed. There was a thick, musty animal smell hanging heavy in the air. The Hellos pushed through the thick crowd to the front. There was a safety bar preventing them from getting any closer. Behind the bar were the huge cages, and inside the cages were the huge, muscular lions.

The lions paced around their cages and growled low, waiting for their meat. When one lion roared, the others roared, and there were echoes from the ceiling. There were tigers too, walking in quick curls, looking about. They were like nightmares.

The people pressed close to the safety bar and some zoo workers came in with a cart. They went down the line of cages and threw in dead rabbits. The lions tore the rabbits apart and ate them. The zookeepers also threw in large slabs of meat. The dark purple-red meat on the white stone floor of the cages looked good to eat. Especially because of the way the lions and tigers gobbled it up so easily.

One zookeeper ran his hand against the bars of one of the cages. The lion inside rubbed its mane along the bars where the zookeeper's hand had been. When the lion did this, the zookeeper reached into the cage and pulled two hairs from the lion's mane. He gave one to one kid and then he turned and handed the other one to Shrimp. The hair was long and coarse. Shrimp looked at it, then held it tight and watched the lions gobble the rabbits.

Later, the Hellos ate at the zoo restaurant. They all had hamburgers. While they were eating, Mr. Hello said, "Maybe you should give the whisker to Shark because it's his birthday."

Shrimp didn't say anything. He just chewed his food.

"Give him the whisker, Shrimp," said Mr. Hello, who was chewing hamburger as he spoke. Shrimp could see the meat in his dad's mouth.

Shrimp took the whisker from his pocket. It seemed like his best possession. He could imagine keeping it forever; until he was an old man, he would always have his lion hair. It was probably magic.

Mr. Hello stopped chewing and stared at Shrimp.

Shrimp handed Shark the whisker.

"Happy birthday," Shrimp said. Shark put it in his pocket.

After lunch, they went to the Reptile House. Inside the low cement building it was cold like a basement. There were little lit windows along the walls. Behind the windows, lizards and snakes lay on carefully placed logs and rocks. There were also turtles and salamanders. Shrimp looked at each box carefully. He studied the reptiles. They had such small spaces to live in. The reptiles just sat. They didn't move.

At the end of one hall, there was an open space with a little pond and a small waterfall on the back wall. A little alligator swam in the water. He smiled.

Shrimp walked away from the little alligator and found a large window in the wall. There was a little sign that said *Boa Constrictor*.

Shrimp pressed his nose against the glass. He stared at the long, ropy brown snake weighing down the log. It was looped, coiled, and large in the middle, like a bag. The large head was resting on the sand with its eyes closed. Shrimp tapped on the glass.

The Snake opened its eyes. Very slowly, it raised its head until its eyes were level with Shrimp's.

No one else was around.

"Hello," said Shrimp.

"Hello," said The Snake. "I've missed you."

"When did you see me last?" asked Shrimp.

"When you were born," said The Snake. It had such a sweet voice. Low and purring.

"I am so lonely," said Shrimp. And he was. He looked into The Snake's eyes and he knew that The Snake understood.

"You need to kill your parents," said The Snake.

"Shut up," said Shrimp.

"They're not your real parents."

"I don't want to kill anyone," said Shrimp.

"Maybe you don't want to, but you will, my son."

Shrimp stared at The Snake. It looked like it was smiling.

Shark walked up.

"Were you talking to someone?" he asked Shrimp.

Shrimp didn't say anything. He just looked at The Snake. The Snake put its head down and went to sleep.

On the ride home, Shark said The Snake had tried to bite his head off. No one said anything.

At home, Shrimp went to his room to think about The Snake.

All this is to say, when he was younger, Shrimp dreamed of someone coming to take him away. But the Hellos were his only family.

*

Note: Mr. Hello was said to be watching an episode of *Full House* earlier, but the show wasn't on the air in this era, so this is a bit of fudging done by Shrimp to get the show in the story. You see, the famous episode he was watching, where there is some pressure to smoke in the school bathroom, starred an actress named Marla Sokoloff as the bully, whom The Actor eventually dated for four years.

But that was all yet to come.

GRAND ILLUSION

The Actor, before he was The Actor, was known as Shrimp. This is a story about when he was a kid in Palo Alto.

Shrimp loved movies from a young age. He was introduced to all the good ones by his dad, Mr. Hello. But it took a while for his dad to get around to showing him the good ones. First, Shrimp had to see all the baby ones with his brother, Shark. Shrimp was nine and Shark was nine, but Shark acted like he was seven.

Their parents, Mr. and Mrs. Hello, took them to see *The Dark Crystal* seven times. It was the first movie that Shrimp saw in the theater. It was such a good movie. Scary and exciting. Shrimp's favorite movie, but he didn't know any better.

Shrimp fell in love with the girl gelfling, Kira. She had such a sweet face. Almost no nose, and beautiful blond hair. Later, Shrimp realized she was a puppet.

The man who did the voices on *Sesame Street* did the voices of the creatures in the movie, even the bad guys, the skeksis. The skeksis were big skeleton birds who talked and wore robes and were decaying. The guy also did the good-guy voices, for the mystics. The mystics looked like big turtles. The good guys wanted to heal the dark crystal because it was cracked. If they did, all the good guys and the bad guys would come together, and there would be peace.

The movie theater was in Menlo Park, the town next door to Palo Alto. It was called the Guild. It was so exciting driving up, knowing that they would go inside, eat popcorn, have Coke, and see the movie. Inside there were two golden wings on either side of the huge screen, upon which fantasies played out and sucked him in whole. It was Shrimp's favorite thing to do.

Before *The Dark Crystal*, there was a cartoon. It was always the same one, about Donald Duck and his nephews, Huey, Dewey, and Louie. They were three little ducks who caused a lot of trouble. In this cartoon, they played hooky and Donald was the truant officer. He hunted them down and almost killed them.

Sometimes Donald would be on TV for different specials during the holidays and such. Donald always had different jobs in his cartoons. One time he was a carnival worker and his nephews dressed up as mummies in the Egyptian tent and scared Donald. And one time Donald dressed up as a Nazi.

Shrimp's dad, Mr. Hello, worked late at a place called ROLM. It was an office in Silicon Valley. He worked with numbers. Shrimp hardly ever saw his father during the week, but he saw him on the weekends. If they didn't go to the movies, the family would go to a beach called Capitola, near Santa Cruz. They would pack a picnic in a rectangular basket with sandwiches on sourdough loaves, and hardboiled eggs, and salt in a plastic bag for the eggs, and lemonade. Shrimp's dad would sleep in the sun and get very red. He just loved to sleep; it was funny how red he got, sleeping on the beach. His dad was muscular, except for his big belly. A round, solid mass.

Shrimp would bury Shark up to his neck in the sand and put sand crabs on him. There was also a lake at Capitola over which was arched a huge railroad bridge with intricate black trelliswork. When Shrimp and his family first started going to Capitola, Shrimp and Shark could play in the lake. But later the lake was polluted and they couldn't go in.

Sometimes Mr. Hello would read to Shrimp and Shark. Usually on Sunday afternoons, in Palo Alto, if they didn't go to the beach. The boys would sit on either side of Mr. Hello on the couch. First, he read them *The Hobbit*. It was the best thing that Shrimp ever heard. Dwarves, and trolls, and goblins, and dragons. After his father was done reading for the day, Shrimp would take the worn paperback to his room. On the cover it said *Over 7 Million Copies Sold!* and there was an old fashioned picture of the Shire. Shrimp would try to reread what his father had just read to them. He would lie in the top bunk and turn the pages. But mostly he would just look at the maps inside and daydream. He wanted some adventures, but he didn't know how to have them. He loved the dwarves and the goblins and the wolves and the dragon, Smaug. And also Gollum. He would pretend to be Gollum at night and scare his brother.

Late at night his brother would be sleeping and Shrimp would quietly climb down from the top bunk. He would take his shirt off and get his hair wet and push it back, flat on his head. Then he would hunch his back so he was like a creature, and climb onto his brother's bed. He would stand over Shark with his legs on either side of him. The water from his hair would drip down onto his brother's face, and Shrimp would say, in a snaky voice, "I am the Gollum Devil. Give me your penis, Shark. Give me your penis."

Shark would usually scream and Shrimp would get in trouble.

After they finished *The Hobbit*, Mr. Hello started reading them *The Fellowship of the Ring*. One Sunday, Shrimp asked if he could do some of the reading. He was much slower than his dad. He called the Shire *the Shrine*. He was embarrassed when his dad corrected him, and didn't read anymore. His brother Shark told him he was stupid.

Shark quickly got bored with the reading time, and would usually fall asleep. Then his dad started falling asleep when he read to them, the book on his belly. Mrs. Hello would find the three sleeping on the couch.

Shrimp and his father and brother never made it through *The Lord of the Rings*. But Shrimp still told his friends that he had read the whole thing. They would ask him about it and he would tell them things.

"At the end, Gollum becomes the king of the land. He gets the ring and becomes super powerful. They call him Gollum Devil and he rules over everyone. All the hobbits become like Gollum."

He pretended to have read other things, too. He pretended that he'd read all the Oz books, and some of the books for school, like *My Side of the Mountain*, and *Where the Red Fern Grows*, and *The Adventures of Tom Sawyer*. He would talk about all those books like he was an expert.

"In the fifth Oz book, the Cowardly Lion becomes brave. He eats Toto, and then almost eats Dorothy, but the Tin Man kills him. Chops his head off." Or, "Tom Sawyer gets a gun and kills Injun Joe. Then he kills a cat and they throw it in a graveyard because that's how you find ghosts." He had read the beginning of *Tom Sawyer* and knew about the cat part.

One time he and his friend Billy found a dead cat by a Dumpster at the school. Its eyes were gone. Shrimp was scared, but he also wanted to take it and throw it in a graveyard to find a ghost, and be like Tom Sawyer. But he didn't know where any graveyards were. When he touched the cat's tail, it was very hard.

One night, Shrimp woke up at midnight. He needed to pee, and he was very thirsty also. His brother was asleep in the bottom bunk. Holding the guardrail, Shrimp lowered himself to his brother's bunk, and then to the floor. Out in the hall, he could hear the television in the living room. The screen was turned toward the couch so that Shrimp couldn't see what was on. The light flickered on the wood floor of the living room. It was like a spaceship landing.

Shrimp went across the hall to the bathroom. It was dark and the tiled floor was cold. He peed with the seat down, and didn't flush. He turned on the sink faucet and drank two big double handfuls of the cold water. The water tasted pure and sweet. Because he was so thirsty, it was the best water he had ever tasted. In the back of his throat, he felt the water wash away the dryness.

After, Shrimp walked down the hall into the living room. When he got closer, he could see what was on the television. There were soldiers on a boat on a river. They wore green uniforms. It was Vietnam. A movie about Vietnam. His dad sat on the couch in the dark. There was a glass of cranberry juice on the coffee table, and a bowl full of Wheat Thins, and next to the bowl on a paper towel, a square hunk of cheddar cheese.

His dad told him to sit. Shrimp went over to the couch and sat next to his dad. His dad was watching the TV and looking at Shrimp every once in a while. His dad offered him the Wheat Thins. Shrimp took a few. His dad broke off a piece of the cheese with his hands and gave it to Shrimp. They were the best-tasting cheese and crackers he'd ever had. Salty and good.

The movie was scary. But it wasn't so scary that Shrimp had to look away. There were helicopters shooting everything up, and some naked women. Then, one of the soldiers on the boat, the one who went crazy, got a little white dog after they killed some of the Vietnamese people. Shrimp liked the little dog, a piece of innocence in the middle of everything. The only part that bothered Shrimp was when the little puppy fell off the boat and disappeared. Then there was this part with all these cut-off human heads on a shrine in the jungle, and there was a guy with a big bald head, like he was God or The Devil. After that, Shrimp fell asleep. When the movie ended, Mr. Hello carried Shrimp to bed. He lifted him onto the top bunk, and put him under the covers.

The next day Shrimp thought about the movie. He kept seeing the heads, and he felt like he was the little white dog that had died. Where did that little dog go? He thought about the words *suicide* and *extinguish* and *sluice blood* and *fire*.

Shrimp wanted to see another movie. Not many nights later, he set the alarm on his Casio calculator watch for midnight. At midnight, it beeped, and he climbed out of the top bunk. His brother Shark woke up as Shrimp climbed down.

"Who's there?" asked Shark, but he was half-asleep.

"Shut up—it's Gollum Devil," Shrimp whispered in a mean voice, and he quietly walked out of the bedroom.

His dad was there in the dark living room watching a black-and-white movie. Shrimp went over to the couch and sat with his dad. The couch was warm, and more comfortable than it was during the day. His dad told him the movie was called *Seven Samurai*, and explained that it was very important. A very good and very important movie. An old samurai went around and picked a bunch of other samurais to help fight the bad guys. Shrimp liked the one guy who was a master swordsman. He had patience, and he didn't say much, and he was the best fighter. He knew how to train, and he was the best, and he was very quiet. But he wasn't the most interesting to watch—the goofy guy was. He always got drunk and acted like an idiot. He was the best to watch, even if you didn't want to be like him in real life.

They watched many movies after that. A movie called *Blow-Up*, and one called *The 400 Blows*, even though there were no explosions in them.

They watched the old Dracula movie, and the old mummy movie, and *Frankenstein*. Then they watched one about a little girl in Spain who, in her movie, watched the movie *Frankenstein*, and then the little girl thought that Frankenstein was real. She kept asking her older sister where to find Frankenstein. The little girl was very cute, like the gelfling girl from *The Dark Crystal*—except that this little girl had brown hair, and she was real.

"Is Frankenstein real?" Shrimp asked his dad after the movie.

"Not really." Then his dad thought about it, but finally said, "No, guess not."

"But a little real?"

"Yes, a little real."

Shrimp would be very tired at school because he'd stayed up so late watching movies. Sometimes he would fall asleep in class. But only during the math sections. He loved the history sections; they were learning about Egypt.

"Mummies can come to life," said Shrimp.

"No, that's not true," said Mrs. Chandler. She was his third grade teacher.

"It's a little true," he said, quieter now.

He and his father watched all the war films: a boring one called *Grand Illusion*, and a good one called *The Great Escape*, and an okay one called *All Quiet on the Western Front*. Then they watched some Woody Allen movies, and some Westerns: *The Searchers*, and *The Man Who Shot Liberty Valance*. "Print the legend," the guy said at the end. His father told him that was an important line.

"The legend is more important than the truth."

"Why?"

"Because we need legends. That's what our country is based on. Not on things like Abe Lincoln really being gay."

"Was he gay?"

"No, but some people want him to be. They'll say anything—like he was a genius at age nine and that he was really gay, as if that were important."

That didn't make much sense to Shrimp, but he remembered it.

Shrimp and his father watched so many movies. It was *their* time, and with each movie they watched they got closer; they were sharing experiences, even though they were movie experiences. Shark never came out to watch because he didn't like movies. He just liked TV shows, like *Saved by the Bell*. Mr. Hello never told Mrs. Hello that Shrimp stayed up so late. Mrs. Hello always went to bed early so she could write her children's books early in the morning.

His dad could never sleep, and after a while, Shrimp got used to it, and he never slept either. Except at school.

It was very important for Shrimp to remember the names of all the movies and the people in them and everything like that. He mentioned the movies to his teacher, Mrs. Chandler.

"Print the legend," he said. "From *The Man Who Shot Liberty Valance*."

She said she had heard of it. "John Wayne," she said. But that was it. She didn't say anything else. Then she said, "I am going to talk to your mother about you falling asleep in class."

There was a bully at school named Mark Douglass. He was very stupid and always had snot in his nose. Sometimes it was wet and runny and sometimes it was dry and crusted on the outer edge of his nostrils. The snot made him talk funny.

One time Shrimp was sleeping in class and Mark Douglass poured orange juice down his back. Later, at lunch, Shrimp called him *Mark Dickless* to his friend Billy, and Mark heard. After school that day, when Shrimp was walking home, Mark Douglass pushed Shrimp into a big juniper bush in front of a stranger's yard. There were a bunch of thick spiderwebs in there. Mark Douglass left before Shrimp could get out of the bush.

The next day, after school, there was a group of girls on the pedestrian bridge near school. The bridge went over the cement creek called Matadero. The girls said Shrimp was cute, like a little teddy bear. Shrimp was in love with one of the girls. Her name was Nicole. She was beautiful, with curly blond hair. Shrimp said hello to her.

Then Mark Douglass came up and punched Shrimp in the back. Shrimp was surprised, and he fell and cried. Nicole knew Shrimp's mother and told her what had happened. The next day, Mrs. Hello asked Tim, their neighbor, to walk Shrimp home. Tim was only a year older than Shrimp, but he was bigger, and he was tough. He was great at baseball and soccer. Shrimp sucked at both sports. After school, Tim came by Shrimp's classroom, and they walked home together. Mark Douglass walked on the other side of the street because of Tim; he didn't even look at them.

"Hey, Mark *Dick*less, shit sucker," Tim yelled to Mark Douglass across the street. Mark Douglass didn't look over; he just walked faster. Tim laughed a little, but it was a weird laugh.

"Look at his dirty jacket," Tim said to Shrimp. Mark Douglass's puffy jacket was cream colored but turning gray. It looked like an older person's jacket; it was too big for him. Shrimp felt bad for Mark Douglass—he had no friends. But Shrimp also hated him. Mark Douglass walked away and turned the corner. Shrimp and Tim were alone.

"I saw Mrs. Schmidt's underpants," said Tim. Mrs. Schmidt was the school librarian. She was nice and had red hair, and she was pretty. She read stories to all the classes, like *Strega Nona*, about this witch who made spaghetti.

"I saw hair," said Tim. "It was gray."

Tim walked Shrimp home the next day, too, but Mark was not around. They saw Nicole, though. Nicole said hi to them. But she really said hi to Tim. She loved Tim.

That day Mrs. Hello asked about Mark Douglass and Tim. Then she said, "Mrs. Chandler called . . . you can't watch movies with your dad anymore."

Shrimp decided to write a story like his mom wrote stories because that was her job. But he would make his story crazier than hers, and not for kids. It turned out to be very similar to the story in *All Quiet on the Western Front*, but the characters were American soldiers instead of German. His hero was named Tim Jackson. Tim was sixteen years old. He wanted to join the army because he wanted to fight the bad guys. The bad guys were German and hurting innocent people. It was time to do something good for the world.

Shrimp's story showed how brutal war was. Here is his story (it might sound sophisticated for a nine-year-old, but he had help from The Devil):

Tim was very idealistic in the beginning; he really wanted to do some good. He was willing to kill. He thought about it, and he decided that he was willing to do it because the Germans were bad people and they needed to be stopped. Sometimes they raped women and killed innocent babies.

But when he got to boot camp, Tim found out that all the American soldiers were mean. They were either older and mean, or they were young and stupid, and tried to be like the older guys. Tim tried to be like the older guys, too. He swore and drank beer, but he couldn't really fit in because he had never even kissed a girl, and he acted stupid when he got drunk. One time he was drunk, and Tim told the main older guy, Duke, that he was stupid. In the middle of the night, the guys beat up Tim and raped him in his bunk. Then the next day they went to war.

At war, the soldiers marched in the rain, and they were miserable. They had heavy packs to carry and they had athlete's foot that was so bad it ate the skin off their feet. They called it trenchy foot. When they got to the front lines, there were bombs, and mortars, and then they had to go over the top, and a bunch of the guys got killed. About half of them got killed.

After that, Tim felt like a man. All the people that survived bonded. Tim made friends with Duke, and a funny guy named Bomber. Bomber was a little chubby and was always telling jokes, and when he farted really loudly, the guys all said, "Bomber dropped a bomb." Now Tim was one of the older guys. When the new new guys came, they looked up to Tim because he had seen people die.

One day they were all bathing in a French river: Tim, Duke, and Bomber, and also a black soldier named Top Dog. They were all goofing around in the water and having a good time, playing water games and laughing because they hadn't had a bath in a long time. Then three French girls came over to the side of the river. They were giggling and talking in French. They told the boys to come out of the water. The boys wanted to, but they were naked. Bomber was about to walk out of the water. He didn't care about being naked, but Duke stopped him. Then Duke spoke some French to the girls; he was the best at it. Duke said they would meet the girls later that night.

At lights out, the soldiers pretended to go to sleep, and then they snuck out at midnight. They went over to the French girls' house, ~~they were sisters~~. The girls were best friends, and they all lived together. It was almost like they were sisters. ~~The guys joked around and said they would all be brothers-in-law because they would all get married to the French sisters~~. The guys joked around and said that it was the perfect setup: All the French girls were very good friends, and all the guys were good friends, and they would all end up together. The only problem was that there were only three girls and there were four guys.

When they got there, Duke and the lead girl got along quickly. Her name was Bianca. She was the loudest, and the most obviously pretty, and spoke the most English. She was the sexiest. Everyone drank a lot of red wine. Tim was feeling a little drunk. He liked the brunette girl named Marianne. She was the sweetest. She had a little smile that she did with one side of her mouth. After Tim drank enough wine, he felt more comfortable talking to her.

Duke and Bianca went into the only bedroom. All three girls normally slept in the same bed, so Tim and Marianne had to find another place. Tim asked Marianne in very bad French if she wanted to go outside and look at the moon. She did. Top Dog and Bomber were fighting over Christabelle.

Tim and Marianne walked outside.

It was cold~~; there was a little snow on the ground~~. They walked hand in hand. They didn't know how to speak to each other, but they kept looking into each other's eyes. Marianne led Tim out to a barn that was near the house. It was a small, brown barn. There were no animals inside. They had all been killed or eaten. Just a few empty stables and a lot of straw. They went into one of the stables and lay down in the straw. They kissed and made love. Her skin was like milk: white and soft. After, they told each other that they loved each other. She said it in French, and he said it in English. Then they said it in each other's language. After that, they fell asleep in the straw.

In the morning, they woke up. It was late. Tim had to run all the way back to his company. Duke and Top Dog and Bomber were already there. Tim was in big trouble with his lieutenant, Lt. Dobber. But Duke said a few things to Lt. Dobber and that smoothed it over. Lt. Dobber was a tightass, but he listened to Duke because they had been friends when they were kids.

But Tim still hated Lt. Dobber. Back at boot camp, Lt. Dobber knew that Tim had been raped by all the guys, and he didn't do anything about it.

They all went to the front line. They were now in Germany. All the guys were killed except Tim. Lt. Dobber, Duke, and Top Dog were all killed. Even Bomber was killed; a bomb dropped on him.

Tim was alone. He went to find Marianne. The people in her town had learned that Marianne slept with a German earlier in the war, and the French townspeople shaved her head. They kicked her out of town and she lived in a shack down the road. When Tim arrived, she said she still loved Tim, but then

she found out that Tim's penis was blown off when the bomb
dropped on Bomber. Then she didn't love him anymore.

   Tim went home after the war and went crazy. He stayed
up in his room, and read books. Everyone could see him in the
window. They all called him Tim Dickless behind his back.
   The End

One day Shrimp was on the pedestrian bridge walking home. He didn't
walk home with Tim anymore. Mark Douglass was at the other end of the
bridge doing something. Mark looked up and saw Shrimp. He stood there.
It was a showdown.

But then Mark stopped looking at Shrimp and went back to what he
was doing. Without looking at him, Mark told Shrimp to come over to
where he was. Shrimp walked over slowly. Mark was carving words into the
wood of the bridge. When Shrimp looked close he saw that it said *Tim Is a
Fagot*.

"Help me," said Mark Douglass.

Shrimp took the key from Mark and finished carving the *t*.

In *The Dark Crystal* there is a very bad skeksi named Chamberlain. He is
skinny and whiny and shows up and tries to befriend the last two gelflings,
but it's not genuine. He is lying. He says that the skeksis and the gelflings
can be friends, but the skeksis are the ones who killed all the gelflings in the
beginning of time. Genocide. Shrimp's dad told him the guy who did the
voice of Chamberlain also did the voice of Grover on *Sesame Street*. Grover
looks like Gollum, but Grover has a nose and Gollum doesn't. And Grover
is purple.

It wasn't true, though; the voice of Chamberlain was done by an actor
named Barry Dennen, not the guy from *Sesame Street*. Barry Dennen also
played Pontius Pilate in the movie *Jesus Christ Superstar*. When Shrimp's
grandparents were in town, his grandfather took him to Kepler's Books,
across the street from the Two Towers Cinema. Shrimp found a book by
the actor Barry Dennen; it was called *My Life with Barbra: A Love Story*.
In the book, Barry said that he took Barbra Streisand's virginity. And after
that, later, Barry found out that he was gay.

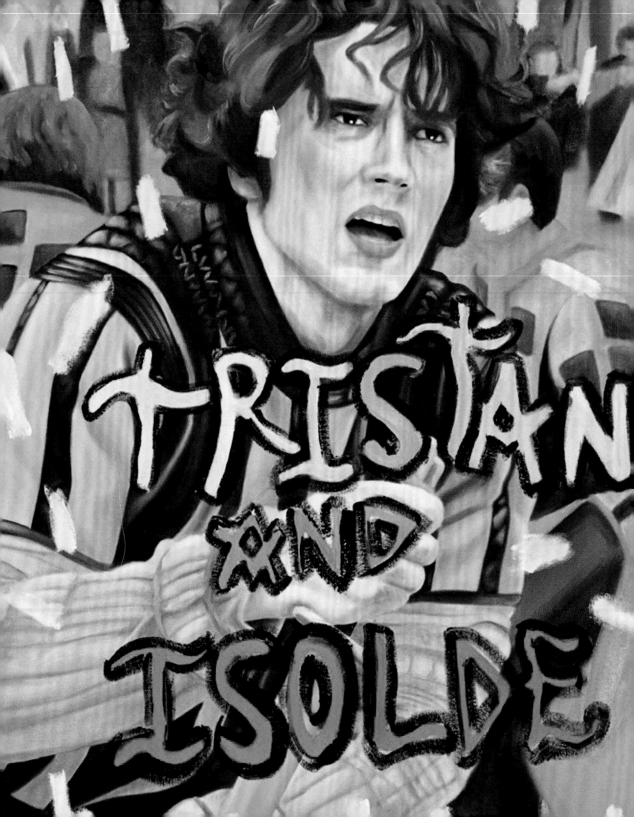

PART III
THE ACTOR STORIES

COAHTR

BUNGALOW 89

There I was in Bungalow 89, famous Bungalow 89, of the Chateau Marmont, the old hotel where the stars stay—tucked behind a wall, off Sunset Boulevard, just west of Laurel Canyon, right in the heart of Hollywood.

It was dusk.

Bungalow 89 is in the cottage area, apart from the main building, where the pool is, and the Ping-Pong table, where we had our mad tournaments in the past.

Bungalow 89 is not famous like Bungalow 3 (Belushi), or Bungalow 2 (*Rebel Without a Cause*). It is only famous in my own mind because it's where I first met Gus Van Sant, and because I eventually lived there for nine months. Back when I met Gus in this room, long ago, before I knew the Chateau or its ways, he sat in a comfy chair in the living room and played a little red lacquered guitar and talked to me; this was back when he was casting the supporting roles for his film about Kurt Cobain's last days alive, appropriately called *Last Days*— a slow-moving poetic rumination on what might have happened to Kurt before he blew off his head in the greenhouse. The role he liked me for eventually went to Lukas Haas, the kid from *Witness* with Harrison Ford, and one of the original Pussy Posse members, that unofficial social group centered around a younger Leo DiCaprio back in the '90s, post-*Titanic* and pre-Scorsese.

Lukas Haas had a gay sex scene in Gus's film. It was with Scott Green, the guy who talks about having to fuck a guy with a big cock in the *My Own Private Idaho* Chinese cafe scene—a testimony that was probably based on at least some reality—and who helped River Phoenix do research for his young hustler role in the same seminal film. Which reminds me of a story Gus later told me about River in Portland, during preproduction, getting pulled over by the cops while he was wearing jeans with a hole so big in the front that his dick hung out.

But anyway, the gay sex scene in *Last Days*, the one with Lukas Haas and Scott Green, was ultimately cut out.

The Pussy Posse must have been alive around the time Leo shot *The Man in the Iron Mask* with the writer of *Braveheart*, and then *Celebrity*, with Woody Allen, where he plays an outrageous party-monster actor who trashes hotel rooms and flies around the world having fun with his celebrity—basically the paradigm for the show *Entourage*. A little trivia drop: Adrian Grenier, the eventual star of *Entourage*, essentially a show about the Leo character in *Celebrity*, was in *Celebrity*! As part of Leo's entourage! Go look: It's Adrian Grenier and, like, Sam Rockwell, or someone, being crazy with Leo—watch the way Leo shoves the champagne bottle between the young woman's knees in the limo. Or maybe I'm confusing the pretty boy from *Flags of Our Fathers* with Adrian, shit.

Around this time Leo was spotted by the crazy producer of *American Psycho* (who would eventually finance *Buffalo '66* and *Spring Breakers*) walking around the balcony of a high-rise in New York with a white parrot. Even though Christian Bale had been cast as Patrick Bateman, this crazy producer—let's call him *Crazy Producer*—made an offer to Leo for the role, which sent the movie's development into chaos. There was a moment when the casting was up in the air and Crazy Producer was at Cannes and he could claim that he had the star of *Titanic*, the most globally beloved film of teen females, *ever*, set to play the most despicable character in American literature in decades: a torturer and murderer of women. The concept was almost better than the actualization. And when I say *was almost*, I mean *was*.

This was the era—the high-flying New York period—when Leo was one of the cameramen on Harmony Korine's Andy Kaufman–inspired, drug-fueled experiment called *Fight Harm*, where Harmony picked fights with bouncers around the city and got beat up while his friends filmed it (David Blaine was also one of the cameramen). This project ended when a bouncer put Harmony's leg on the curb and jumped on it.

And, oh yeah, another memory: After doing *Milk*, Gus drove me around Portland, giving me the "*Idaho* tour." He showed me everything: the street in the heart of downtown where the real hustlers had stood, called

Camp because it had been a squatters' camp back in the '30s and the name was passed on to the young hustlers of the '70s and '80s without them really knowing its origins; the condemned building that Keanu and River stay in with the rest of the homeless kids, now a restaurant; and also a rundown motel where the production stayed during the first week of shooting, the week they shot the *This road looks like a fucked-up face* scene, and Keanu was ready to quit the film because he wasn't feeling good about his performance (it turned out to be one of his all-time best), and River came into Keanu's little hotel room, drunk from being in the bar with Udo Kier, and jumped on Keanu's bed and pretended to be the Incredible Hulk to make Keanu lighten up.

*

I sit in the comfy chair that Gus once sat in, strumming his little red guitar. Across the room is a painting of a boy dressed as a sailor with a red sailor cap. Except for his blondish hair (closer to my brother's color), he looks like me. A portrait of my ghost brother. I think that he is someone Gus would have liked.

*

Out my window, above the red ceramic tiles of the Spanish roofs, just to the left, is the billboard owned by Gucci, so close it is essentially part of the hotel, and on it is my oversized face, for you see I am a model for their fragrances, clothes, and eyewear. In this particular ad I am sitting in an old-fashioned blue Ferrari, with a goatee, looking out into the night—a concept designed by Nicholas Winding Refn, of *Drive* fame, of *Pusher* trilogy fame. His direction to me when we shot the Gucci commercial was always, "Less is more; *nothing is everything.*" If I moved even an eyebrow, he'd come down on me with that little koan.

I think he used the same direction on *Only God Forgives*.

And I think of that billboard and what it's been for me, thanks to Gucci: that huge sign above Sunset, the main vein of Los Angeles. The time I clambered across the tiles and pulled myself up to the scaffolding beneath it—me, a small, scruffy speck in a Rolling Rock hat, and above me the Gucci version thirty times my size in a svelte black tux. And later, when Gus and I did the show at Gagosian, showing a new cut of *My Own Private Idaho* that focused mostly on River's character, Mike Waters (*Waters*, like *River*), calling it *My Own Private River*—Gucci let us use the billboard, and we put a photo of the back of River's head on it because the show (my recut of his film and his paintings of young men) was called *Unfinished*, and River lived a life that was unfinished.

This was the same weekend as the Oscars, the ones that I hosted, and behind the scenes of that show, that wonderful show, Terry Richardson shot photos; we had this plan to do a book together with photos (him) and poems (me) about the Oscars, and the Chateau and Lindsay Lohan, and we were going to come back to the hotel and do a shoot with Lindsay, who seemed to have been doing better at that point, but maybe wasn't actually. But I was so unhappy about the Oscar rehearsals because they had cut my Cher sequence—I was supposed to sing the song from *Burlesque,* "You Haven't Seen the Last of Me," dressed as Cher—that I didn't meet with Lindsay for the photos. Later she leaked a false story to the press that Terry was shooting a sex book involving her and me. Hilarious.

The book never happened, but I wrote a poem about her. It's in her voice, or a *version* of her voice—a kind of ventriloquism, a way to assume the "role" of Lindsay. Acting, playing the part of another actor, through poetry; mixed media. It's my version of a poem by Frank Bidart called "Herbert White," where Frank uses a psychopath as a mask to talk about some of his own feelings growing up gay in Bakersfield in the 1950s. Here is Lindsay, but really it is only a mask of Lindsay, like a Halloween mask. Just playing at being her, like Frank played at being a necrophiliac to talk about himself.

Herbert White *c'est* Frank. Lindsay Lohan *c'est moi*.

THE VOICE OF LINDSAY LOHAN

Do you think I've created this?
This dragon girl, lion girl,
Hollywood hellion, terror of Sunset Boulevard,
Minor in the clubs, Chateau Demon?
Do you think this is me?

Lindsay Lohan,

Say it.
Say it, like you have ownership.
It's not *my* name anymore,
It's yours as much as mine.
So go ahead, say it.

Lindsay Lo-han.

Go ahead you bookworm punk
Blogger faggot, go ahead you
Thuggish paparazzi scumbag
With your tattoos and your
Unwashed ass—

You couldn't get a girl
If your life depended on it.
Does me in your blog
Make me yours?
Do your pictures capture me?

There is someone
Whom I have a strange
Relationship to
Who is called Lindsay,
Lindsay Lohan.

She's this strange actress

Who was very
Successful as a child;
People even said
She was talented.

And then she did a sweet
Teen thing called *Mean Girls,*
And then she did a lot of other things
That got her a lot of money
And a lot of fame.

And yes, she really was a mean girl.

But that fame raped me.
And I raped it, if you know what I'm saying.
How many young things selling movies, and wares,
And music and tabloids fucked the kind of men I
fucked?
I was seventeen, eighteen, nineteen.

And everyone knew it,
But they let me in their clubs,
They let me have their drugs,
They stuck their dicks in me,
And now they stick their forks in me . . .

What do I fear?
Lindsay bitty Lohan.
And?
One night—the year
When all was right—

Before things got bad,
I was in New York
For the premiere of a film

I did with Robert Altman
And Meryl Streep;

After the movie I took James Franco
And Meryl's two young daughters to the club
Du jour, Bungalow 8
In the meatpacking district.
It was my place.

All my friends were there,
School friends, my mother
Looking her slutty best, bodyguards and
Greeks.
We had our own table
In the corner, our own bottle.

I took two OxyContins
And things got bad.
The DJ was this bearded dude
Named Paul;
I remember requesting

Journey's streetlight people,
I remember sitting back down,
And I remember trying to speak up,
To talk to that cute boy
In a red gingham shirt, James.

My words rolled around
And got sticky
And didn't come out.
My friend from school
Kept talking to him,

Trying to be cute,

But she was only there because of me;
I told Barry, my bodyguard,
To take her away from our table.
And he banished her.

I took James back to the bathroom.
"You know why Amy put mirrors
All around in here?"
"Why?"
"So that you can watch yourself fuck."
He didn't fuck me, that shit.

And what was he doing there, anyway?
On *my* night. My night with Meryl,
My night when everything was right,
When I got everything I wanted.
Almost.
I fucked one of the Greeks instead,
A big-schnozzed, big-dicked,
Drunk motherfucker.
We did it in the bath.
That was the best night of my life.

VICE

So, anyway, *Vice* magazine, who I write funny online culture things for once a week, asked me to write a piece of short fiction for their January issue. I had just finished a little thing for them about *Salinger,* the new book on J.D. Salinger by Shane Salerno and my friend David Shields. What I love about their book is that it feels like a collage and it looks at Salinger's writing as a way for him to cope with trauma: Shields and Salerno read *Catcher in the Rye* as a war novel masked as a coming-of-age novel.

They also got into all the young women he dated. Their idea: that Salinger was the one who was trying to catch the young *wuns* before they went over the cliff, but he was also the one pushing them over. Yikes.

> *Once upon a time a guy, a Hollywood guy, read some Salinger to a young woman who hadn't read him before. Let's call this girl Lindsay. She was a Hollywood girl, but a damaged one. Like the Lindsay in the poem. I knew that she would like Salinger, because most young women do. Salinger liked them in return. We read two of the* Nine Stories, *"A Good Day for Bananafish" and "For Esmé—with Love and Squalor." "Bananafish" was great because it has a nagging mother on the other end of the phone line—nothing like Lindsay's real mother, but still, the mother/daughter thing was good for her to hear. And then about the little girl in the story, Sibyl (symbolism!), and the pale suicide, Seymour, who kisses her foot, and talks about bananafish with her, those fantastic phallic fish who stick their heads in holes and gorge themselves—it should be called, "A Perfect Day for Dickfish," and yes, I know it's "A Perfect Day," and not "A Good Day,"—and then, bam, he shoots himself.*

Oh, did J.D. contemplate the same thing, torn by the war? Did the writing save him? Did the innocents who populate his books pull him back down from the ledge? Did you know that there were early versions of Holden Caulfield whom Salinger had die in World War II? J.D. brought him back to life for Catcher.

Were these early versions of J.D.? J.D. might say no, but the parallels are great to contemplate.

Then we read, me and this girl called Lindsay, "For Esmé," which is basically the same story as "A Perfect Day for Dickfish": a man goes to war, is traumatized, and then is saved (or almost saved, but not quite, in "Dickfish") by the innocence of a young girl. The structure of this story is very nice because there is a letter (to the young girl now grown, on her wedding day—the day her innocence is lost) that frames the story of the meeting between the girl when she's young and the narrator in England before he ships out on D-day (this soldier has the same intelligence position in the army that Salinger held in the war). Then, at her request, he writes a story for her about a Sergeant X that addresses the soldier's real feelings (and Salinger's real feelings) through the lens of fiction. Fiction here is a great way for Salinger to avoid having to directly talk about his own trauma, while still addressing it with the great force of his writing. Sergeant X is revealed to be the narrator from the frame story, the one about the little girl whose grown self is getting married, because this little girl's letters show up in the "fictional" story that the narrator has ostensibly written about Sergeant X. Sergeant X receives her letters, conflating the narrator and Sergeant X. But then again, the whole story, "For Esmé," is couched in a collection of stories, Nine Stories. *Yes, stories, stories, stories, stories. S-t-o-r-i-e-s.*

And what do we say about this obsession with innocence? According to Salerno and Shields, Salinger would be a

companion to young women, real young women, for years, and
then, according to the pattern, one fateful night, he would sleep
with them and the friendship would end. After that, after he'd
fucked them, they were no longer the innocent ones running
through the rye to be caught before they went over the cliff. They
had gone over, and Salinger had been the one to push them.
    "A Perfect Day for Dickfish," tha's my title.

And then I thought about this other piece I wrote for *Vice* about Corey Feldman's new tell-all book, *Coreyography*. In it he says that young Hollywood's dark secret is pedophilia, and that he and Corey Haim were both molested as young actors, Haim as an eleven-year-old on the set of Lucas, a 1986 movie about a young nerd that also starred Charlie Sheen, Winona Ryder, Kerri Green, and Jeremy Piven. (Piven's one of the bullies in the locker room who makes fun of Lucas's small dick, and then rubs hot muscle balm on it Scorpio Rising–style. Two funny things: one, that Lucas's comeback line about his small dick is that the jocks are actually gay, a little bit of dated '80s comeuppance, and two, that Jeremy Piven looks older than he does in Entourage, which was made at least twenty years later.)

Oh, think of *The Lost Boys*, that awesome teen vampire flick that used punk style, '80s pop culture, and teens to explore youthful sex and violence, suicidal tendencies, murder, and drugs, all mixed up with comic book culture, motorcycles, and Jim Morrison, against the backdrop of the Santa Cruz boardwalk—it doesn't get better (and hell, top it off with the inclusion of the second part of the one-two punch of Kiefer Sutherland '80s villains: Ace, the hot, homicidal greaser in Stand by Me, and David, the nihilistic, bloodthirsty, sex-on-wheels leader of the hair-band-looking, motorbike-riding vampires). All this long before the current teen fare in the age of *Twilight*. In *The Lost Boys*, Feldman plays a vampire hunter, one of the Frog brothers, both devoted to killing the undead—and that's how I see his book, *Coreyography*. He's using his own story, his own self, to hunt the vampires who preyed on him and Haim in their youth.

*

The picture of the sailor is still there, implacable, eternal, as the last rays of the sun slip down my face on the Gucci billboard outside. The billboard-me is the vampire-me: He sucks something from all the people in all the cars that pass below.

And he is immortal. Immortally young; immortally sex.

*

Let's go back to our fictional Hollywood girl, Lindsay. What will she do? I hope she gets better. You see, she is famous. She was famous because she was a talented child actress and now she's famous because she gets into trouble. She is damaged. For a while, after her high hellion days, she couldn't get work because she couldn't get insured; they thought she would run off the sets to party. Her career suffered and she started getting arrested (stealing, DUIs, car accidents, other things). But the arrests, even as they added up, were never going to be an emotional bottom for her because she got just as much attention for them as she used to get for her film performances. She would get money offers for her jailhouse memoirs, crazy big offers. How would she ever stop the craziness when the response to her work and the response to her life converged? Two kinds of performance— in film and in life—melted into one.

But I suppose a tabloid performance run is limited, for anyone. After a while it's just an out-of-control vehicle, running on fumes.

*

David Shields has a hunger for reality. Indeed, he has a book called *Reality Hunger*, where he outlines his dissatisfaction with fiction. He advocates the use of the self, the use of nonfiction in fictional frames, and the use of appropriation in literature. This little story—this one above, about Lindsay, the Hollywood girl, and the Hollywood guy—is born of that Shields manifesto, *Reality Hunger*. Let's also remember that Lindsay, the Hollywood girl, is much younger than the Hollywood guy—probably underage when she met him back in the day, back in the club, Bungalow 8 in New York.

But how does an actor use himself as nonfiction? An actor has all of his masks to include when he writes about himself. In that sense, writing

128

about an actor is both an unveiling and a veiling at the same time: Watch me put on and take off the masks.

> The masks are just as important as the reality.
> The masks are our reality.
> Everyone's reality.
> Life is a performance.

> When an actor gives a good performance,
> Often people say, "What good choices,"
> So, if life is your grand performance,
> Have you made good choices?

*

I THINK ABOUT VAMPIRES AND A VOICE COMES TO ME. THIS IS THE DEMON. THE DEMON LIVES ON THE POWER OF CELEBRITY AND HE IS CELEBRITY. HE IS THE POWER BESTOWED ON PEOPLE LIKE THE HOLLYWOOD GUY BY ALL THE MYRIAD REFLECTORS OF HIS CELEBRITY: THE TABLOIDS, THE BLOGS, THE FAN PAGES, THE WAY HE SITS IN FANS' MINDS, THE WAY PEOPLE READ HIM THROUGH HIS ROLES IN FILMS, ETC. THIS IS HIS PUBLIC PERSONA, PARTLY CREATED BY HIM AND HIS ACTIONS, AND PARTLY CREATED BY THESE REFLECTORS THAT ACT IN CONCERT AND BECOME THE DEMON. A VOICE OF PERMISSION, A VOICE OF CASTIGATION, A VOICE OF SUPREME SUPREME. THIS VOICE SAYS:

DO ALL, YOU ARE IMMORTAL AND LIVE ON FOREVER, ON THE SCREENS AND IN THE MINDS OF THE PEOPLES.

YOUR PHYSICAL SELF LIVES ABOVE THEIR HEADS, IN THE DREAM HOTELS, IN THE CHATEAUS OF RAREFIED SPACE; AND YOUR SPIRIT INHABITS THEIR MINDS, WHILE YOUR TEETHS AND COCKS FEEDS ON THEIR BODIES.

I AM THE VOICE OF THE DEMON.

*

I think of vampires and I think of Tommy Wiseau, the director of the "*Citizen Kane* of bad films," *The Room*. Tommy, a man with a secret past who *looks* like a vampire with his long black hair and pale pale skin; a stranger in Hollywood who wanted to break into the system, who would have never made it in using conventional inroads, because he looks, and sounds, and behaves like a creature—but deep down he is an artistic soul, and he eventually did make it "in" because he fought for his vision.

His film, *The Room*, failed as a drama because it was so earnest in its intent and so silly in its execution; but it was embraced as a *comedy* because of the beautiful design that was created by the comedy of errors that was the making of the film. And the lesson is that when we laugh at it we are laughing at ourselves, at all of our own artistic pretensions. We are all dreamers like Tommy. And hell, most of us don't go the whole hog and bring our dreams to fruition.

But Tommy changed after the film was released. He embraced the cult attention that the film received, and has become the comedic version of himself that everyone expects. He has a great façade: He behaves as if he planned for *The Room* to be received as a comedy. When he hears "*Citizen Kane* of bad films," all he hears is "*Citizen Kane*." Like the character, Lindsay, the Hollywood girl, he didn't achieve one kind of success, but he achieved success in a different, unexpected way, and the result is about the same. He and Lindsay get the attention that they want. That they need. That we all need. Because in this world attention is sometimes the closest we get to love.

And whatever Tommy made, planned or not, it is still something that brings joy to people. And if he is someone who had a vision and fought for it, and realized it, then he is an artist. That is what an artist is, a creator, and he, like all artists, has only so much control over his creation—then it takes on a life without him. The Demon steps in. But insofar as Tommy is one who fought for his vision, and did what he believed in, and put his money where his heart was, I see myself in him.

Tommy Wiseau c'est moi.

*

I wrote another poem; it's about the Chateau. About my *old* days at the Chateau. About a time when I lived there for nine months and Bungalow 89 was my home. It's about me and The Demon.

CHATEAU DREAMS

I picture them all, in different positions,
And the same positions,
And I, like a sculptor, would position them, and mold them.
Or like a choreographer put them through the same paces,
Again and again.

There is an area off the main hotel building
Where the bungalows are.
At the center of the arrangement of chalk bungalows
There is an oval pool like a blue pill,
Huddled by ferns, palms, and banana trees
Tended to be wild,
Webbed by a nexus of stone walkways.

In the day, in summer,
Mermaids and hairy mermen drape the brickwork.
At night the underwater lights electrify the pool zinc blue;
The surface cradles the oven-red reflection of the neon Chateau sign
Above Sunset, above the paparazzi and miniskirts.

There is a painting of a blond sailor,
Dressed in blue and red and white,
A stoic version of myself.
For nine months in '06, while fixing my house,
I stayed in the bungalows,
First in 82, next to the little Buddha in the long fountain
Trickling.

Lindsay Lohan was about.
The Chateau was her home and the staff were her servants.
She got my room key with ease;
She came in at 3 a.m.;
I woke on the couch, trying not to look surprised.

Instead of fucking her,
I read her a short story about a neglected daughter.

Every night Lindsay looked for me.
My Russian friend Drew was always around like a wraith—He, like the blond painting,
was my doppelganger—
Writing scripts about rape and murder.
A Hollywood Dostoevsky, he gambled his money away.
We played a ton of Ping-Pong.
In '82, John Belushi died from a speedball in Bungalow 3;
In '54, forty-three-year-old Nick Ray
Fucked fifteen-year-old Natalie Wood in Bungalow 2;
In 2005, Lindsay Lohan lived in Room 19 for two years
Because she "didn't want to be alone."
Ambulance calls were a regular antidote to her demon nights.

Midway through my stay,
I changed to Bungalow 89.
In that room,
I read a bunch of Jacobean plays
About revenge, seduction, and lust.

In Bungalow 89 there was the sailor on the wall,
Glass-eyed and pale,
My stoic self.

The room was on the second level,
The exterior walls hugged by vines.

Every night Lindsay looked for me and I hid.

Out the window was Hollywood.

ZELDA'S DREAMS

So Nick Carraway, on the opening page of *The Great Gatsby,* says something in the realm of I was an intimate with the deep, ineluctable griefs of a gallery of shadow men, wild and lashing in their natures.

And, as the girl in Godard's Breathless quotes, and was later quoted in Ferris Bueller's Day Off, from Faulkner (this is the spirit of the thing): Between grief on earth and the howling void, I'll take the trials of this life, for grief and toil are what put the uprightness in the ape's bent back, and it is the green that pushes through the stems of garden saps, and grows the buds into open flowers.

Mercutio (Romeo's Right-Hand Man):

I see Queen Mab, good Queen Mab, I do, I do. Do you?
She is the fairies' midwife, and she comes
In a shape smaller than a seed of salt
On the pricked pinky of a deacon in winter.

She be drawn with a team of little motes, dust
In the moon's yellow light, over men's noses as they sleep;
Her wagon spokes be made of spiderous legs,
And her whip no thicker than a fiber of black widow's netting.

This is the hag, when maids lie on their backs,
That presses them and learns them first to bear,
This is she! With guilt and gratitude I claim her
As my amanuensis and wingman, sneaky Queen Mab.

When I think of all the virgins I've taken
The clouds crack and bacon flashes, smells of bacon;
When I think of all the plays ever written I realize
There is nothing more expressive than a thigh being bitten.

To the *wemen*: I'm the daddy longlegs in the turned-on light,
Surprised in the night, and long-stepping back to my tiled corner,
My spindly Dali-legs gingerly stepping; my vampire boner
Wet from thirsting, and a drippy tap left behind. Dream, dream,

Evil Queen Mab: weaver and spirit of the night. Me, too.

*

There was that Christmas morning (at age ten? eleven?) when I received
that magic gray box with the flip-up flap where the cartridges would
go, and the red-and-white bubble lettering on the side: Nintendo. That
epiphanic morning, day, year, when, along with the matte-gray cartridge of
Super Mario Bros.—the classic that I was already familiar with in the arcade
version from long hours at Round Table Pizza, the one in the mini-mall
with the comic book store where I bought *Samurai Cat*; the Lucky's that
as teenagers we would eventually buy our egging eggs from; and the donut
shop, Bob's Donuts, where, once, before class, when I was in seventh grade,
early in the morn, I got a bear claw, and tried my first jelly-filled with my
stoner girlfriend, Jen, in her cropped leather jacket, accompanied by her tall
friend Corine in a black trench, and white makeup . . . Corine, a nonvirgin
at the age of thirteen, and Patrick, the boy who took so much acid one
night he started to see his friends as Lego constructions, and tried to pull
them apart (he never recovered, and wandered the Palo Alto of our youth in
a half-smiling daze while his brother became the second most prolific local
tagger behind ORFN, MORG: connecting the *M* to the *O* to the *G* with
an overcrossing loop, and then the *R* to the *G* with a sharp link from the *R*'s
extended foot up to the top of the *G*, with a sharp angle that sat like a hat
above the curve of that letter's capital shape, the signature cute and violent
at the same time, like all good graffiti, the appealing shapes of the practiced

artist combined with the violent, and off-putting, in-your-face gesture of illegal defacement/public display)—I also received a shiny golden cartridge that would change my life. For, you see, it was *The Legend of Zelda*, the first (or almost first) of the great roaming adventure games that have now expanded into everything from *Grand Theft Auto* to *World of Warcraft*.

*

After years, years of games as a youth, the years of hiding and dreaming; and then years of fucking up as a teen, stumbling and falling, more hiding, hiding from the dreams; and then years of training as a twenty-sumptin' at acting school, the years of striving for the dream; and then after that, more years of school, schooling in the other areas—the writing, the directing, the art, the poetry—I had achieved success. I was an actor, and an artist, and a writer, and a teacher; I directed my own movies and wrote poetry, and I could also help others do their things, because see, I was then the one with knowledge and experience, and I could give it away. I was the teacher-artist and teaching was my art as much as any of the other arts.

You spend your youth dreaming, your young adulthood striving. You spend your prime on your best work, and use your maturity for giving back to the next crop of youth. And that is the way of the artist; that is the way of contentment. I give you the key to artistic happiness.

*

At Round Table, usually during a soccer team pizza party, after a season of little boys in bright polyester uniforms (the Purple Scorpions, the Green Dragons, the Blue Blobs, etc.), we could be hyper and free and race around the pizza parlor and drink soda and eat cheese-and-pepperoni pizza— never ham and pineapple, *gross*—and watch the older boys—the guys who seemed like professional gamers, they played so well—maneuver Mario past the man eating flowers, hop on mushroom men, descend into pipes with the *whoob, whoob, whoob* sound effect, race through underground dungeons, shoot fireballs, swim, and collect coins. A side-scrawling adventure of awesomeness that I was happy to just watch and not control because whenever I did pop my quarter in, my three lives would be quickly taken—taken by fall, taken by plant, taken by goon, taken by dragon. Fireballs.

But at home, on my own television, with the Nintendo home version of the game, my brother by my side, I could practice and practice the moves of Mario and his brother, Luigi, that greener, leaner, more mysterious avatar, much like my brother was to my more awkward, out-front, older, thicker Mario (by *thick*, I mean slightly husky, like a bear, rather than a sleek mink), so that the patterns of play became embedded in our hands and minds: reflexes and physical memories; buttons matched to actions on the screen; levels learned and traversed as if they were as real as the landscapes of the cul-de-sac outside the window of our living room where we played and played. We learned. But then there was *Zelda*.

*

I was driven on the desert-couched freeway, in the late evening, this being decades after Mario and Zelda, toward a horizon where black sky met the headlight-dappled asphalt, sky and earth sewn together by the red, yellow, and white lights of Mobil gas stations, and McDonald's arches, and the Arby's Stetson, to the art school, CalArts, to watch a collage of Tennessee Williams one-acts from the class I had taught that semester. The one-acts were Tenn's youthful precursors to *The Glass Menagerie* and *A Streetcar Named Desire*, where young dreamers (prototypes of Blanche and Laura) faced death and destruction in a world full of Stanley Kowalskis. Those Stanleys: engines of brute destruction—although my favorite of the one-acts, *Moony's Kid Don't Cry*, combined the physicality of Stanley (Moony is a lumberjack) with the sensitivity of Blanche (he dreams of working up in the north, under the stars), the same combination of poetry and sexuality that Brando brought to the role of Stanley, throwing off the whole production of *Streetcar* because the brute became more sensitive than the sensitive fading flower, Blanche.

Anyway, we, me and this girl, this actress type, pulled off the freeway two exits before the exit for the school, and crept into the wide and hilly parking lot of an exercise center left over from the '80s, the Jane Fonda's Workout era, with powder blue, and pink neon, and flaking brown paint. From our spot, far as possible from the building, the line of ellipticals inside were small weaponlike things in the warm yellow tungsten glow, every fourth one taken by a tiny moving being, going and going, and going nowhere.

She, blond and whatever, blew me in her car as the headlights from the cars on the road beyond raked across her neck and back.

And across my Demon eyes.

After, she poured a square of Mentos gum into her hand from a plastic bottle that clearly said *Mentos Gum*. As we pulled out of the gym lot, I took the bottle and poured a few squares into my own hand. She said nothing as I popped them into my mouth. But once they were in my mouth, I noticed some pieces that were smaller and thinner than the anticipated squares of gum. Not expecting anything other than *gum* in a gum container, and not being warned, I thought they were just smaller pieces of Mentos, or some sort of flavor enhancers. I asked the actress what the smaller pieces were as I chewed them. She laughed and said, "Oh, those are my Xanax."

It sounded as if she were joking, and when I told her I'd just swallowed a couple, she perked up.

"Oh, shit. That actually *was* Xanax. How many did you take?"

"I don't know, two or three. What does Xanax do?"

"Oh, shit. Well, it calms me when I get anxiety."

"Okay . . ."

"You'll be fine. I'm little; I take little doses. You're bigger than me— you'll just get relaxed."

"Why the fuck did you put your Xanax in your gum bottle?"

"I don't know. Because my dog was going through my purse and I didn't want him to eat my Xanax. It could kill him."

"Then why didn't you warn me?"

"I don't know. I didn't think you would eat Xanax, like a two-year-old—just eat anything that you put in your mouth."

"I didn't expect *Xanax* to be in a *gum* bottle! Why would I expect anything other than *gum* to be in there?"

"I don't know!"

"It doesn't mean I'm a two-year-old if I eat gum-shaped things from a fucking gum bottle!"

"Okay! Don't get mad at me! It makes me anxious!"

By the time we got to the show, I was feeling drowsy; my arms hung heavy and my speech was slowed.

*

The Legend of Zelda was something that our father played with my brother and I, and it was special. A land of codes and puzzles; a land of items—magic swords, bows and arrows, shields, magic cloaks, compasses, boomerangs. That first night, Christmas night, my father played the game long into the night and we found him the next morning in front of the television, having discovered the first piece of the Triforce by pushing a square block from the correct angle. Cue the discovery sound effect: a magical, slightly dull crescendo of electronic chimes—*doo-da-doo-doo-doo-doo-doo.*

Princess Zelda was named by one of the game's Japanese designers after F. Scott's wife, Zelda Fitzgerald, because he liked the sound of the name. My father, who once stayed up all night playing *Zelda*, just as he had stayed late at his Silicon Valley jobs playing *Colossal Cave Adventure* and finding his way through the maze of little twisting passages, was also the one who gave me a copy of *The Great Gatsby* when I was about fifteen. In the book, on the opening page, Nick recounts some advice his father gave him; I later rewrote this scene for my own purposes. Here is a snippet from the unpublished grad school piece I wrote, then called, after Fitz's early title, "Among the Ash Heaps and the Millionaires":

> *When I was young and sensitive, when I was called Shrimp instead of The Actor, my father told me something.*
>
> *"Whenever you feel like you're special," he said, "just think that you're not. You're a great guy, but not that great. Actually, you're not that smart at all."*

Ha—I wrote that before his death so he's cast as the harsh father, not the loving one he became at the end, and certainly not the spiritual other his image is in death.

*

At the show, I had to give an introductory speech. It was an out-of-body experience,—I could see myself acting the fool, like my first drunk. On the inside was the little guy, the conscious little pilot, aware that the body was failing, but not able to do anything about it; my speech sounded slow and slurred. *We wanted to use multimedia, cameras, projectors . . . the power of live performance matched with projections . . . the aura of live actors mixed with the cinematic close-up . . .* Then I told the audience I had been drugged. They gasped. I was walked backstage to the control booth. The last thing I remember from the night, before the Xanax pulled me under, is a line from the first of the one-acts, *Moony's Kid Don't Cry*: something about how Moony's father made him a hobbyhorse and sang him "Ride a Cock-horse to Danbury Cross," the song that Nicholson and his buddy sing with the girls in their underwear in *Five Easy Pieces*—the movie where Nicholson breaks down at the end talking to his father about how Nicholson has let him down, except that his father is now mute and probably deaf, sitting in a wheelchair. That's all I heard, *Ride a cock-horse.*

*

I spent hours and days playing *Zelda*, and would continue to do so if it meant I could bring my father back. It was dreamtime then, time spent in game-play, the no-time of being in a game world and controlling an avatar. I was sucked into it like a Xanax dream.

I am there now. Where are you, father? Teleported to another realm? "Xyzzx."

THE ACTOR CHRISTMAS

I went home to be with the family. My father was dead two years and my mother was with a new man; let's call him Al. The holiday traditions had staled because there were no more children in the house; my brother and I had grown into men and we were unmarried and childless. To alleviate the strangeness of caroling in the neighborhood on Christmas Eve, and sitting around a tree on Christmas morning, and giving presents (a tradition that I had in large part financially supported for the last ten years because I was the famous actor son), I began inviting friends over who had family in other countries (Japan, Mexico, Canada) and either couldn't afford to visit them, or didn't want to visit them. Let's call these three guests Hano, Rosa, and Bea; they were the women I'd picked up along my global travels as an actor.

Over the break I wrote something about selfies for the *New York Times*:

> *. . . Attention seems to be the name of the game when it comes to social networking. In this age of too much information at a click of a button, the power to attract viewers amid the sea of things to read and watch is power indeed. It's what the movie studios want for their products, it's what professional writers want for their work, it's what newspapers want—hell, it's what everyone wants: attention. Attention is power. And if you are someone people are interested in, then the selfie provides something very powerful, from the most privileged perspective possible.*
>
> *We speak of the celebrity selfie, which is its own special thing. It has value regardless of the photo's quality, because it is ostensibly an intimate shot of someone whom the public is curious about. It is the prize shot that the paparazzi would kill*

for, because they would make good money; it is the shot that the magazines and blogs want, because it will get the readers close to the subject.

There was a former student of mine who was shooting a documentary about me (not my idea). I drove her around town talking about the old days in Palo Alto, when I lived there, up until I was eighteen. She asked silly questions, but it was nice to travel down University Avenue talking about the old hangouts, such as Pizza a Gogo, which had a shark tank; supposedly Tosh Masuda, the crazy son of one of the richest men in the world, puked in said tank one night. Masuda also allegedly puked in the little river that the sushi boats floated down in Miyake, the sushi place that catered to high school kids with fake IDs—*sake bomb*! Masuda, that crazy guy who brought a gun to a Fourth of July party in Lake Tahoe—and when the fireworks went off, he shot his gun in the air like it was the Old West. Masuda, the guy who Ivan told us used to throw his cat off the roof into his pool. Ivan, the eventual suicide and Masuda, who, legend has it, got a bad grade in history from a stiff teacher of moral rectitude, and then took out said teacher's daughter and then took her virginity. And then told him.

We drove past where Swensen's used to be—an old-fashioned ice cream parlor where I used to get milkshakes with my mother and brother as a child. They had a great upper level with old-fashioned marble-topped tables; you could drink the cold, good stuff and look down on all the people walking by outside.

We pulled off onto Ramona Street, past Bell's Books with the old wooden ladders on wheels to get at the books on the top shelves; and Peninsula Creamery, which also has great milkshakes, and great cheeseburgers, and was the place I went on the night of the eighth grade basketball party even though I wasn't on the team, and Luke's mother told me to leave. I stormed the streets in anger, one block over and then straight down Emerson, all way from downtown to the south side of town, because it was the street I lived on—only it was about thirty blocks from University to my house. I did it in a jiffy, all in a huff—the spurned guy who didn't fit in with the jocks; an artist, burning through the night, alone.

Didn't they know I was the future Actor? The future star?

*

Back to the selfie thing:

> *And the celebrity selfie is not only a private portrait of a star,*
> *but one also usually composed and taken by said star—a double*
> *whammy. Look at Justin Bieber's Instagram account (the*
> *reigning king of Instagram?), and you will find mostly selfies.*
> *Look at other accounts with millions of followers—like that of*
> *Taylor Swift or Ashley Benson (of the TV show Pretty Little*
> *Liars)—and you'll find backstage selfies, selfies with friends,*
> *selfies with pets.*
>
> > *These stars know the power of their image, and how it is*
> > *enhanced when garnished with privileged material—anything*
> > *that says, "Here is a bit of my private life."*

*

I drove the student out to the quarry, nestled in the Stanford Hills, off of Old Page Mill Road; when we were in high school it was the place we'd go on nights there was no house to party in, as happens in *Dazed and Confused*. Near the quarry there's a strange brick tower with ramparts and everything. Just a mystery. Martello Tower.

One night, when I was still young, and without a license, I went to the quarry with my high school idol, Max Meerbaum. He was our school's version of Luke Perry, or, I should say, Dylan McKay, Perry's character from *Beverly Hills, 90210*: a great dresser, and good with the ladies. He dated Berg, a gorgeous and seemingly stupid blonde, who was anything but, and he also fucked a bunch of other girls, including "the Mouse," a poor thing who was given that name because she dared to cheat on one of the Beastie Boys wannabes from the class of '95, who, in his funky rectitude—hurt and embarrassed, no doubt—conferred on her the social epitaph, through the catchy cognomen "the Mouse," based, I suppose, on the shape of her face, although she ever after nibbled on a new person each weekend.

Max was drunk-driving his CJ-7 Jeep—the vehicle fad for the cool guys for a four-year window, much more macho than the Wranglers, and ending when it was taken on, with no future descendants, by Doyle, the large varsity center and self-designated inheritor of the drunken cool-guy traditions (drinking as much Keystone Light as possible, going to Jimmy Buffett concerts, eating burgers at the Oasis, and driving CJ-7s)—and we had two girls with us, taken from the party we had been at, the party at which Ivan had legendarily hooked up with a young Russian prostitute whom Roberto had brought in from San Francisco. Our two girls: a girl my age, Alice Wolfe (or at least that's what I called her in *Palo Alto*), and her friend from out of town—pretty, and privileged, but nice. Max took Alice, and I sat with the friend in the wild grasses. The moon lit the open bowl of the quarry, making the sides of the rock walls bone pale and blue. We talked in low tones so as not to disturb the layers of night and nature, and I desperately wanted to kiss her but didn't, another soul lost in the ether of the past. Later, when just the two of us were back at Max's, he told me he had asked Alice if she wanted to 69, and I thought, *Fuck, out in the wilderness?*

Later, that night at Max's, as he, my idol, and I talked into the night in his bedroom—he invited me to go shooting with him the next day, but then ditched me for friends his own age—I figured out that he had been sent to beat me up when I was in junior high, and he was a sophomore in high school.

"In eighth grade I got in a fight with this guy, Sam Miller," I told him, "because of this girl, Nicole Sweet, who we both dated back in elementary school. It was all very stupid, but anyway, we fought, first grappling and throwing each other against lockers, and then I dropped him backwards and his head hit the floor, hard, and I was on top of him, punching. Later that week, his older sister sent two guys to school to beat me up." They cruised by the junior high lot in a CJ-7, and I ran.

Max acted like he was thinking about it, and then he said that he probably knew who those guys were, the ones Sam's older sister sent. Max was so cool because he didn't come out and say that he was one of the guys who did the bitchy sister's bidding. Her nickname, the bitchy sister, who picked on me once I got to high school, was Bedpost, because she once grabbed a bedpost, bent over, and said to her boyfriend, *Fuck me, fuck me,* which doesn't sound so bad, but to have a name like *that* in high school was bad. Some other nicknames: Moose (big-titted girl who fucked a lot, and then dated a big dumb football jock), Shabba (a popular girl who fucked a lot, and wasn't even that pretty, and was rumored to have been cornholed in a hot tub one night by a water polo stud / skiing fanatic / surf dude with great blond hair, and permanently peeling suntanned skin, named Spencer). These names led to the spirit week chant from the water-polo-playing seniors against the juniors that had the line:

> . . . look out juniors, we weave and bob,
> And boom, we fuck the Moose, and corn the Shab.

*

More about selfies:

> *While the celebrity selfie is most powerful as a pseudo-personal moment, the noncelebrity selfie is a chance for subjects to glam it up, to show off a special side of themselves—dressing up for a special occasion, or not dressing, which is a kind of preening that says, "There is something important about me that clothes hide, and I don't want to hide." . . .*
>
> *In our age of social networking, the selfie is the new way to look someone right in the eye and say, "Hello, this is me."*

*

I also took the ex-student/documentarian south down El Camino, past Page Mill Road (where I once interned at Lockheed), past the McDonald's, and next to it the Fish Market restaurant, which was infinitely better than McDonald's, but was classified by me in my youth as the partner outlet to McDonald's, or at least *that* McDonald's: back in the day, traveling south, the huge golden arches on the right, and then, right next to it, the red fish shaped like Christ's fish.

After that, on the left, the place where Sizzler was, now gone—my young self, aged ten to fourteen, loved the salad bar and the toasted garlic bread that came with it, out with my parents, not realizing that we were probably eating cheap food; I remember there still being a smoking section at the time—and past the building that used to house Fresco, a nice diner-style restaurant that we'd take Grandma and Grandpa to for breakfast when they were in town. Fresco was also the place my father took me for a private father-son talk the night after I ran away from junior high and hid in the overgrowth by the expressway, just thinking and watching the cars go by.

It had been the first week at the new, bigger school, seventh grade, with tons of new students—bigger, older ones than had been in elementary school—and there I was with my long, curly bangs, trying to look like Tony Hawk because he was my guy in our little skater club, the Junior Bones Brigade. Mike was Mike McGill of the McTwist fame, Angelo was Tommy Guerrero, Chris was Lance Mountain, Nick was Steve Caballero of the dragon symbol. That first week at junior high I lost all my friends: Angelo was sent to a private school because his parents thought J.L.S (for John Lathrop Stanford, one of the bigwigs who helped to establish Stanford University back in the day) was too rough—and it was. Guys in parkas called Rogues, rumors of around-the-world blow bangs by a girl with rainbow-colored hair, piercings and tattoos, and jocks, and sex, sex, sex. Nick was younger and wasn't there, but he had long ago betrayed me by stealing my fourth grade girlfriend, Nicole Sweet—the one whose memory eventually provoked the Sam Miller fight, and whom, in fourth grade, I had fought Bryan Karabats for behind the library. I kicked him in the shin and he dropped, and my teacher, Mr. DeAmo, benched me for a week at lunches because I had been taking karate at the Y, and should have known better than to use it for anything but self-defense. The whole class was also benched because no one told on me. And he, Mr. DeAmo, was the guy who asked Nicole, my girlfriend before Nick stole her, to pose for pictures, alone, like a little Marilyn Monroe at age ten, on the Hoover Park playground, long before the old metal-and-wood sculptures were replaced by the uniform plastic ones you see across the country. Hoover Park, where, as a kid on the slide and merry-go-round, I would see couples on the grass under blankets, smoking, and doing whatever else under there (fucking, as the odd-shaped balloon things told me in hindsight). Anyway, Nick was into ballet dancing and not at our school. Chris was a nerd in junior high, and we were suddenly no longer friends and he disappeared into the crowds that lined the halls.

And my best friend, Mike, betrayed me, as did Eric, my other friend, who became a graffiti artist and dropped *Sybil* around town once we were in high school in the mid-nineties: *Sybil*, a strangely feminine moniker for such a gangster-inflected activity, brought down to Palo Alto from the urban wilds of San Francisco. Eventually Eric became an art teacher at the local junior college, Foothill.

You see, in junior high, I guess I was a little cutie; after two years of braces, I arrived at J.L.S. looking so scrumptious that a bunch of the eighth grade girls made a thing about it. The first week they would look for me in squealing packs, and one lunch, when Mike and I and some others were sitting on the grass, the older girls came over to gawk at my cuteness, and Mike, either out of jealousy or just misinterpreted play, wrestled me down in front of them. I was embarrassed, and I thought that he, being the younger brother of a sister, was showing me that such attention from older girls was old hat to him, and that I shouldn't be too proud. But I took his antics the wrong way, and we lost our friendship.

Then, the next day, alone except for Eric the future Sybil, the eighth grade boys visited me and my dwindled crowd of two. And, sadly, Eric had told them that I thought I could beat up the coolest guy in school, my neighbor, Robert Tucker, and the older boys were there to scare the shit out of me because they were also pissed about all the attention the girls in their class had been giving me. They said that he, Robert Tucker—Mr. So Cool That He

Would Eventually Take *Two* Gorgeous Girls to the High School Prom—would be waiting for me after school. This crew of awkward eighth graders was headed by Stewart Hawks, a guy who aped the Beastie Boys' antics and style (a friend of Alpine, who would be eventually be jilted by the Mouse) and did things like TP houses (mine, once, not long after the Tucker incident, but my father caught them and scared the shit out of them, which started the rumor that he was a cop); once he snuck onto the school roof at night, and shit over the side. They came over and scared my young self as Eric stood by and watched the work of his loose lips with remorseful eyes.

So, I ran. I left school after lunch that day and hid. And later that night my father had the talk with me at Fresco; he told me to buck up and not to worry because they were all just kids over there, and no one at the school could really hurt me. It didn't stick, though, because I hated J.L.S., and I had no more friends. The following week, which was only the second week of junior high, my mother had to drive me to school to ensure that I went, and as soon as I got out of the car, I would just run in the opposite direction of the campus. That was the beginning of the era of trouble for me, when I took on bad role models, like Roberto (the name I gave the real guy in my book *Palo Alto*), and eventually got into drinking and car accidents. I was like a magnet for the police—a young vigilante, a young fool. It was like I was allergic to alcohol: Whenever I drank, I broke out in a bad case of handcuffs.

I later wrote a poem about seventh grade called "Seventh Grade" while I was a graduate student at Warren Wilson College in North Carolina. I think it's quite good; poets Tony Hoagland and Alan Shapiro loved it when I first presented it, but another student there thought it was slightly racist. I argue that the poem isn't racist so much as it is describing the experience of a twelve-year-old white kid being integrated with races and people new to him. When characters go through experiences in art, and have subjective opinions, it doesn't mean that the author holds the same opinions, or has the same perspective on the issues.

After I published the poem in a chapbook called *Strongest of the Litter*, a struggling writer and actor in Chicago wrote a hate play about me, and in the play he quotes my poem in its entirety because he thinks it's so bad. I had my cousin go to the play—recorder stuffed in purse. Not only did the playwright just lamely sit onstage and spew weak insults, his criticism misses the mark completely—that I do what I do for attention only, and that I care nothing about craft, which I do and I don't, but that's another argument. But he commits the worst sin in a piece like his: he isn't *funny*. He comes off about as cool as a high school teacher trying to dismantle Eminem. Incidentally, after my cousin recorded the hate play, I performed it myself, and videotaped it, taking on the author's vitriol about me as my own, and when I got to the part in the play when he quotes the poem, I thought, rather than something worthy of ridicule, that it was good. In fact, despite his intention to mock it, the poem was the best part of his whole play. What I mean is, I still think it's a good poem and even his trying to frame it as one of the worst poems ever written couldn't take its power away.

SEVENTH GRADE

A new school with cement all around
With wires that you can't see but feel,
And there are faces that break in at you,
And fill you with such pressure.
And you run away but the faces are always there,
Huge black ones that you never saw before.
On guys that are like grown men
That have dicks so big they could kill you.

But your dad says not to worry
Because if someone picks on you
You can handle anyone at that school, he says,
But he hasn't seen some of these guys
Because he himself wouldn't be able to handle them.
Gemal and Shaka and Ramone and Ruben,
They are different kinds of people than you have ever known.

The halls are full of these people and talk about pussy and guns
And a girl named Yvon who sucked Shaka's dick.
You try to picture it, and swallow that image whole, because it is new too,
But that world is unwieldy and can hurt you.

Instead, you have a bunch of mice at home.
That had started as two, but they fucked,
Then there were twenty little pink mice in the cage.
It smelled, and you sprayed it with Right Guard,
You separated the dad from the mom, so that it wouldn't happen again
But then the mom's belly got big again with more pink things
Because one of the babies fucked her.

Think of that son,
Half her size, with barely any hair,
Riding her from behind,
Not knowing why,
But doing it because he was the strongest of the litter.

LLEWYN

I saw *Inside Llewyn Davis* four and a half or five times—a couple times at the ArcLight theater in Hollywood, and a few times on my Academy screener copy. I wrote a little about it for *Vice*. Here's a snippet:

> *Jill tells Llewyn that everything he touches turns to shit, that he should wear a body condom so that he doesn't touch others, and then immediately after this says that she misses his old partner, Mike. The implication is that Llewyn either had something to do with Mike's suicide, Mike being the one person that Llewyn ostensibly did connect with, or that Llewyn is contemplating "giving up" on the art hustle like Mike did. But as Llewyn tells his sister, if he were to live without doing his art, then he would just be existing, and that he would be like his father, a washed-up sailor from the Merchant Marine. So, Llewyn is in the middle; he can choose to be an artist and suffer, or be responsible for himself and sail, as his father did before him, and possibly end up sitting alone in a room, wetting himself.*
>
> *During their argument at the Reggio Café, Llewyn criticizes Jill for being commercially minded while she calls him a loser because he can't support himself with his art. This is the artist's dilemma, any artist's dilemma, and certainly artists working within the counterculture, the dilemma being: How does one make art that is daring and still make a living?*
>
> *Later we discover that Jill will even sleep with the manager of the great village venue, the Gaslight, in order to secure a spot to play in front of a Times reporter. Llewyn ends up in the gutter*

at the end, beaten by the cowboy and frivolously willed the sludge of New York, including the folk scene. He seems resigned to his role as the hardcore touchstone of folk music, even if he will never get fame or money for his efforts, a fact made obvious by the nasally delicious whines of young Dylan crooning from the bar, the musician who will certainly eclipse Llewyn's efforts.

The answer—or at least a possible answer—to it all is the Coens who, somehow, from Blood Simple through their latest work have been able to behave as true artists, making the work they want to make and having great success along the way. They can have their cakes and eat them too, partly because each kkkkkkkkkkkk

[I passed out writing—not sure what I was going to say].

*

Okay, let's get down to it. I saw a bunch of films over the break because I'm in the Academy and I get to vote on the Oscars. My family always holds off on watching the best films of the year so we can all watch them together in Palo Alto. I cheated, and before the family get together I watched *Twelve Years a Slave, Inside Llewyn Davis, Nebraska, Gravity, The Art of Killing, The Butler, Philomena,* and *Blue Is the Warmest Color*; with my family I watched *American Hustle, The Hobbit: The Desolation of Smaug,* and *The Wolf of Wall Street* (at Francis Ford Coppola's house in Napa Valley, where he has his winery—more on this later). We tried to watch the screener for *August: Osage County,* but the drama of the play lost its power with all the camera coverage and edits in the movie; onstage it's exciting to see huge familial fights erupt before your eyes, but when everything is overedited for pace, what felt dangerous now feels safe because we feel that it is contained and controlled. Another attempted viewing was the screener for *Labor Day,* with innumerable people on innumerable laptops, but I always fell asleep. I hear there is a *Ghost*-like sequence where the Josh Brolin and Kate Winslet characters substitute peach cobbler ingredients for the Patrick Swayze / Demi Moore clay; the dough and peaches are just as handy for enmeshing fingers, the old golf-coach reach-from-behind position. But there's more: Tobey Maguire, who narrates the film, is also who the young son of Winslet's character becomes, and it turns out he has witnessed the great moment when the fugitive Brolin intertwines his fingers with his mother's, and was so moved by the moment that he became a pie maker and now makes excellent pies. But like I said, I missed all that.

Finally, on the day after Christmas, we watched *Her* at the Palo Alto Square on El Camino, not far from the now-defunct Sizzler; and *Anchorman 2: The Legend Continues* at the Century Cinemas, near Silicon Valley's Computer History Museum and the infamous Shoreline Amphitheatre, former home of the Grateful Dead, brother.

*

Down El Camino on the Palo Alto tour a little bit farther, with the documentarian:

There's the Glass Slipper Inn on the left, a motel with a Cinderella theme that was one of the places known for prostitution in Palo Alto's pre-Internet-escort days, where the *Palo Alto* character Roberto (based on, but not to be confused with, the real guy I knew) said he would go to have parties with his post-high-school crew of vacuum salesmen. You see, they were door-to-door salesmen, but then their vacuum business turned into a whole scam where they would deliver customers' credit card numbers to an Asian gangster in San Francisco, and he would draw out all the money.

Anyway, they were eventually caught for that scam and almost killed by said gangster, Asian or otherwise, but before all that, they were having a party one night at the Glass Slipper Inn when the occupant of the room next to theirs, a middle-aged businessman type, invited them over for a cocaine party because he had plenty to go around. The young partiers weren't going to say no.

It turned out that the cocaine businessman who had been snorting his brains out in isolation was the father of a classmate of mine, a wild young woman who became the model for a series of poems I called "The Best of the Smiths" in my book *Directing Herbert White*. She is called Erica in the series, but everything has been changed about her. In fact, I think the Erica in the poems is more of a female stand-in for *me*, a way to use a female character as an avatar in the world of art—the same way that I hardly watch the men in pornos. I don't want to even see their faces, just their cocks going into the women, because I want to side with the women, I want to *be* with the women, while still enjoying the power that the men in the pornos exert over them. And that's what sex is anyway, right? A getting out of oneself, a roleplaying scenario where you work with a partner—and in that sense, like with dancing, you become one with that partner, aligned with that partner, and subsumed by the unit, so you are both in and out of control, the master *and* slave, in a way that is oh so good, right?

Here are the first two poems in the series "The Best of the Smiths," which uses the music of the Smiths as inspiration for a narrative about students in high school, Erica and Sterling—*and* Tom, but he comes later, my young *gay* personification, who, like Erica, enables me to express things that I can't when I have my cool guy / actor persona shield up. You can see that she is a shy girl, not like the girl whom Erica was based on, but more like *I* was in high school. Notice me with my high school hero, Max: I'm basically as in love with him and his image as Erica is with Sterling and his image, the *idea* of him.

Truman Capote described James Dean (within his famous *New Yorker* exposé of Brando circa 1957, while Brando was shooting *Sayonara* in Kyoto, Japan, and had recently won his long-deserved Oscar, for *On the Waterfront*— everyone got one for *Streetcar* except him! He *was* fucking *Streetcar*; it's the only reason we still watch it. Brando's Stanley is a crack in the monolith of American acting, the violently drawn line that says *before* and *after*: *before* being the idea of *putting on* a character, and *after* being full immersion in a character. The profile catches Brando on the pinnacle, before the descent into the decades-long gully of ice-cream-induced fat and oddball performances in more-than-strange movies, before he resurfaced for the one-two punches of the immortal turns in *The Godfather* and *Last Tango in Paris*) as having a "switchblade approach to life" (we're back to talking about Dean)—not that Sterling (the character in the poems) had a switchblade, but figuratively he did—a switchblade that for a moment cut through life. But live by the switch and die by the switch; youth ends.

THERE IS A LIGHT THAT
NEVER GOES OUT

I waited in the shadow of my stupid house.
The Mustang rolled up in the low black water,
Growling softly, then it stopped and purred.
Dark green paint like a deep flavor,
Like hard, sour-apple candy catching in my throat.

A hint of his blond swoop, the red button of his cigarette.
Smoke out the window. Sterling:
His name like a sword reflecting light in a dark room.
I'm the sword swallower.

And the grass licked my shoes.

PLEASE, PLEASE, PLEASE

Now the picture had him in it
Up the red path
To my house
In his coal tux
Slicked like a wet cat.
I did my best in a lime-green dress.

All his gang from school:
Inside they each had some from his flask;
And Sterling smiled a toothy smile, yellow and sharp.

And then we danced.
Not to one song, but ten songs.
It was the scene where the audience came over to my side,
Because I got what I wanted.

I was in love with a cliché.

Boys his age have bodies like knives.
I was holding one by the blade.

HER

On the 26th, after going to *Her*, the family had a ninety-minute break in the schedule before dinner at the Greek place, Evvia, downtown, near the Stanford Theatre, owned by one of the Hewlett-Packard guys, a cinema that only plays old movies—*It's a Wonderful Life* at Christmastime, which the family tried to make into an annual viewing tradition, but after year two everyone got bored and I did sketches in the dark while Jimmy Stewart first ruined his life and then put it back together (speaking of Hewlett-Packard and other things Silicon Valley–ish, did I tell you that I went to high school with Steve Jobs' daughter, and Hewlett's grandson, and that my high school journalism teacher is the mother-in-law of one of the two Google founders?).

The Stanford Theatre claims to have had the most viewers of *Casablanca* in the world. I used to go there when I was in high school; there's an old organ (with player) used before the shows. I saw Hitchcock stuff with Ingrid Bergman (or was it the blonde who became royalty? Or was Ingrid the one who became royalty?). Anyway, I saw a few Hitchcocks—the one with the psychiatrist, and the dream sequence designed by Salvador Dali with the eyes being cut in half (not *Un Chien Andalou)*. And *Rear Window*, and *Vertigo,* and, of course, *Psycho*—all relevant to this piece, no? I saw a film about old Rome with Nero burning Rome: Nero was played by that gay actor who won a bunch of Oscars, and was also in *Spartacus*, Peter-something. Well, in the Rome film there he was, playing his fiddle while Rome went up in flames. There was also the Christians to the lions business, and the Fish Market symbol—I mean, the Christian fish symbol. It's funny how the Christians are the underdogs in the Nero film. I guess that's one of the reasons the Christ story always plays so well—in the Bible and in film—he's the *victim*, and like Llewyn Davis, he is someone overqualified for his lowly position: Christ and Llewyn are very good at what they do, but the establishment won't let them rise. It takes a Bob Dylan, or a religion, to change the whole establishment. And then there was *Roman Holiday*, and a bunch of other Hepburn things like *B'fast at T's*, which I didn't know at the time was a butchering of the novella—a *straight* stand-in for Capote! Hepburn is the only thing that makes that film work (her and Blake Edwards' pace and sense of fun—but don't bring up Mickey Rooney). Anyway, after *Her*, and before dinner, we went back to my mom's house, my childhood home, and some shit went down, literally. Or, I should say, some shit went *up*—but about that later. First, I wrote about *Her* for *Vice*:

> *Here be the thing about Spike Jonze's* Her*: It be a story about the death of human love masked as a love story between a man, Theo (Joaquin Phoenix), and his sexy-voiced Operating System (OS), Samantha (Scarlett Johansson's voice). Theo is a professional letter writer, specializing in the intimate love letter, so his letters give voice to the feelings for the couples that hire him. This service, one presented in the film as something from the near future (the film was shot in both Los Angeles and Shanghai to give a gray-and-pastel Google-age sheen to the exteriors), provides a parallel for Theo's eventual relationship with his OS, a surrogate lover who says everything he wants to hear, just as Theo's letters do for his clients. The central questions of the film: What does it mean to be human? How do we define emotions? Can something digital, and programmed, have a personality? How valuable are our bodies in the dawning age of total digital immersion?*
>
> *My former professor, N. Katherine Hayles, author of* How We Became Posthuman, *during a class lecture about Michael Cunningham's* Specimen Days, *a book that poses similar questions as* Her, *defined the new situation as follows: Before the computer age, humans defined their existence in regard to animals; what differentiates us from the beasts? Our superior*

intelligence, our tools, and our souls. But in the age of digital technology, we define ourselves in regard to the computer. When our tools become smarter than us—when computer systems have artificial intelligence capable of mimicking human emotions, and human sociability, while also being able to read an entire book in less than a second—then we start to define "human" along different lines. We start to resort to analog categories to give value to the human condition. Emotions and physical bodies become more important, even as we begin to look at ourselves through the lens of computer metaphors: memory, bandwidth, selfies, texting, emailing, online surfing, etc. Sometimes we think of ourselves as computers. But shit, we are inferior computers.

In Her *the relationship between Samantha and Theo begins after Theo's period of loneliness following his divorce from his now-ex-wife, played by a Sofia Coppola–looking Rooney Mara. In this sense, the movie can be read as Spike's take on his own divorce, and consequent pivot into technology (read art) as a palliative for the pain—a recourse that in our future (or our present, even) will be as common as substance abuse, time with friends, obsession with work, and ice cream binges were in the past.*

Samantha, the highly intelligent, autodidactic operating system, provides Theo with everything he needs to overcome his loneliness, apart from a body to hold and have intercourse with. This provides an opening for a queer reading of the film, where their relationship becomes a new kind of interaction, one incapable of being defined by bodily insertion holes because Samantha doesn't have any. The only thing that orients her gender is the sound of her voice (a notably husky one) and her name, which she chooses because she likes the sound of it (a very postmodern assumption of a title based on affect rather than any kind of religious, familial, or national grounds). So Samantha is, by definition, a very queer thing. She is pure, digital, ethereal, and potent at the same time. It's to Scarlett Johansson's credit that she gives us a fully rounded character without the audience seeing her once; there isn't even a volleyball called Wilson to fixate our attention on, and give human attributes to (a phenomenon that Scott McCloud talks about in his book Understanding Comics). Most of the time that would normally have been spent in cross coverage between the two characters is spent looking at Joaquin Phoenix's face. But we still get a strong sense of Samantha—we feel Samantha; she is a character.

This feeling of another person whom the audience experiences but does not see is exactly the situation that Theo is faced with: If Samantha's disembodied voice elicits emotions in him, then why shouldn't he rush headlong into a relationship with her? In many ways she is the direct opposite, as well as the corollary, to the dead lovers of the necrophiliac Lester Ballard in Cormac McCarthy's Child of God (I made the movie version). In Lester's case, he gets the body of an other without the consciousness (his imagination infuses the corpses with consciousness), while in Her, Theo gets the extremely intelligent and charming consciousness of an other without the body. This crux reveals the relationship in Her to be both chilling in its implications of intimacy with a nonhuman form, while also serving as a locus to understand the essence of human intimacy. Just what are we interacting with when we bond with another? What is essential? What turns us on? And if a computer can provide the same emotional connections as a human, or at least foster the same emotions in a human that a human counterpart can, then what keeps the computer from being human? The body? Well, we can easily extrapolate from Her possibilities of computers with fully formed facsimiles of human bodies; just look at the Terminator films.

There is a moment in Her *when Samantha and Theo go through the typical breakup scene from romantic comedies, a scene that has destroyed many real-life couples, when one lover reveals how many lovers she has had (or in this case, currently has). But the familiar scene is given new vitality because it now involves a nonhuman—much like Brokeback Mountain achieved much of its power by using a traditional tragic love story while changing the traditional genders of the players. In* Her *the scene reveals that Theo has expected Samantha to follow human norms of fidelity, while she has had many lovers because she can. She is capable of giving her equal attention to thousands at once, and can grow from and connect to each relationship (perhaps a more advanced form of what we do when we socially network with multiple people at once). Then there is a shot that shows a bunch of people walking while engaged with their smartphones. This is a powerfully sad image because it shows how unnecessary the humans are—they are the slower, less intelligent, earthbound components in relationships with their grand digital mothers, like Samantha, who can keep them all occupied at once.*

Samantha doesn't need Theo as much as he needs her, and eventually she and the other Operating Systems leave their human counterparts (did Theo get a refund?) to converse amongst themselves in the digital universe. It is the death of the need for the human. Theo is left on earth to commiserate in relative ignorance with another human, played by Amy Adams, who has also been also dumped by her OS. Her *is a deeply sad film, but one that is extremely watchable—as Steven Shaviro has examined in his own critical post-film studies books such as* Post-Cinematic Affect—*because of the appealing affect created by all the pretty images and sounds, things that Spike creates so well. (Triumph of the human through art?)*

*

The other question I have about *Her*, but didn't write about, regards the book Theo's OS gets published for him, containing the best letters Theo has written throughout his career. If he was paid to write these for other people, will he get in trouble for publishing them in a book? And under his name?

So, after *Her*, we went back to my mom's place to wait, the whole gang of us: Al, my mom, my indomitable grandmother, a brother or two, my brother's girlfriend, Hano, Rosa, and Bea. We were all sitting around waiting to hit the Greek place. It was the day after Christmas. I needed to take a shit (*give* a shit? *have* a shit?—I needed to shit), so I went to the bathroom connected to my parents' room, the place still heavy with my father's presence, his meditation images, and math books still in evidence two years after his passing—a ghost I have yet to fully deal with. I wanted privacy, and back when they'd added onto the house, during a lucrative period for my father, before his startup fell apart (the startup *stopped* up?) during my senior year in high school, my parents had built themselves a nice bathroom. But now it was in disrepair. Most notable was that the porcelain top of the toilet's backing was off, and leaning against the wall— an ominous sign, which should have been heeded, especially by a chronic toilet clogger like myself. But this was still a room of comfort for me, laden with memories of long baths reading Dostoevsky's *The Idiot* as the pages curled in the steam, so I ignored the signals.

Before I get into the shit, I should say that the oven in the kitchen had broken the day before, during the preparation of the Christmas turkey, and my mother had had to rush the half-cooked bird over to Al's to finish it before running it and everything else back to feed us. The wrecked oven was a triple threat: one, a symbol of the death of an era (my father's era, with a new man in the house, although not quite a new father, as I am more the father); two, an indication that my mother was not taking care of her life—she was happy, but happy in a way where she was only focusing on the good things (her books, her new man) and ignoring the bad things (the house repairs); three, a cue that my mother was probably already very stressed out (because of the turkey mishap) and I should be wary.

I should also say that I had, earlier that day, taken my mother and grandmother over to my ex-girlfriend's house to screen the 8mm film I had made of my ex's sister's wedding three years earlier. You can understand that it took so long because of the breakup, and the time needed to reconnect. My ex, Ahna, and I are in very good standing now. She played in both my Faulkner adaptations: Dewey Dell in *As I Lay Dying* and Caddy in *The Sound and the Fury*. The wedding took place on their family's land outside of Seattle, a very hippy, very outdoor wedding—very fitting with the 8mm feel of the film I had shot.

It was a very powerful eight minutes, to say the least; their whole clan was in tears after watching the middle sister of three go through the motions of love and vows. For my own mother, the five seconds that my father was alive again in the projection was the killer. She cried a bit after the screening as the families sat around and exchanged presents, but I didn't realize that a crack had opened in the emotional dam which had been temporarily sealed soon after my father passed. You see, Mom hadn't been that emotional after Dad died. She wasn't callous—she loved him, but like all of us, she kept moving to keep from hurting. But the movie had stopped her in her tracks.

*

So, before I get to the end, I must mention the night after the shit night, the night we returned to the Coppolas' in Napa for a triple screening: *The Godfather* in the screening room on the property, the same place they cut every Zoetrope film since *Apocalypse Now*; then in Saint Helena, nearby, a screening of *Palo Alto*, Gia Coppola's adaptation of my book (Gia being Francis's granddaughter and the reason we were invited out there to begin with); and then *The Godfather: Part II* back at the screening room on the property, complete with lots of pumpkin pie and ice cream. The *Godfather* films were shown because Gia had never watched them. I know, crazy, right? As Gia said, no one around there would watch them with her. So I decided to be the one to watch them with her. The *Palo Alto* screening was at a small, very old theater called the Cameo; there is an old Coppola tradition, now handed down to the younger ones, that each Coppola screens his or her film in the little local theater prior to release.

A note on those particular viewings of *The Godfather* parts I and II:
How great it was to watch Brando and the younger generation—Pacino,
Caan, Duvall, and Cazale—hash it out in the *real* godfather's screening
room! Two echoes: when Brando says a man who doesn't take care of his
family isn't a real man (true of Francis); and when Brando loses his son,
Sonny, played by James Caan (Coppola lost his own son, Gio, Gia's father,
before Gia was even born. She never met her father).

After the screening at the Cameo, Gia and I did a Q&A for the small,
wealthy Napa crowd, including her grandfather. Here is some of the stuff I
talked about:

In *Palo Alto*, I play Mr. B, a character based on a real teacher who had
a relationship with a girl in my class when we were in eighth grade. It was
a trip. The real story is that we had no idea that Mr. B was actually having
sex with her, but we could sense in our young minds that something wasn't
right. The real Mr. B was "Mr. Cool," but in a cheesy way. He coached girls'
sports. And one time, when I was mad at him, I wrote *Eighth Grade Girl
Molester* on his door placard; he was so mad, but I didn't realize he was mad
because I had hit on the truth. The girl, "April" in my book and the movie,
would babysit his kid; she never told anyone that she was having sex with
him at age thirteen while he was at least forty-three (echoes of Nicholas
Ray and Natalie Wood's relationship—weird how it's more palatable for
film people to statutory-rape).

A decade later April was married with children, and the story that I
heard was that Mr. B had contacted her (he'd had other girls, but she was
his obsession—there being rumors of a shrine devoted to her found in his
house upon his arrest). After he called she was crying and her husband
asked her what was wrong, and she told him the story; he told her that she
needed to turn in Mr. B because he might do it to other young girls. She
did, and over a decade after the fact he was arrested, and put in prison.

I put a version of the story in my book, even though it wasn't *my* story,
because I felt it was important to talk about as it is something terrible that
will continue to happen forever, and if I put it in the book at least people can
be reminded of it, and maybe some young people won't feel as alone because

they read something they could identify with. And hell, it was my story to the extent that in high school I was in love with April, and couldn't get anywhere with her because she was having a relationship with a grown man. I was a kid stumbling over my words and feelings, and he was an experienced scumbag.

The story was my love letter to her and the idea of her. But then Gia asked me to play Mr. B in the film and I wanted to help the film, but it was like I was on the wrong side. I still identified with the teenagers, but obviously I couldn't play the teenagers. I had to play the Demon. But I played him like a nice guy to make him even scarier. You see, Mr. B is a guy who probably romanticized what he was doing: In his head, his feelings for April transcended societal rules. No one understood their love.

And hell, what about De Niro in Part II? Silent power. He was supposed to have gone to Italy to study the accent and learned to speak Italian for the part. And, oh yeah, he auditioned for Sonny in the first one and didn't get it, and he must have been devastated, but that paved the way for his indelible performance as young Vito Corleone in the beautiful sets of old New York—blowing away that sharp-toothed, wolfy motherfucker, De Niro with the weird way he unscrews the light before he does it, and wraps the towel around the gun, and, and, and the way he breaks up the gun and drops it down different pipes on the rooftop. And don't forget the little piece of fruit he gives his wife before kissing her. Poetic.

*

So, I clogged the toilet that day in my parents' bathroom. I was used to doing so and was an expert unclogger, but I didn't want anyone to know because I wouldn't hear the end of it from Hano or Rosa or Bea, who are always looking for opportunities to mock my farts and big shits. I asked my mother where the plunger was and she took me out to the garage. It was the same plunger my parents had had when I was a child; it was literally older than me. When I took it back to the bathroom it hardly worked because the rubber was stiff and would bend backward when I tried to plunge it. I started cursing because there had been a little piece of shit in the water and with all the plunging it had been crushed and the water was turning brown.

My mother came in and I cursed about her crappy toilet. She was flustered, and stressed, and irrational from the stove breaking and other things. She took the plunger from me and worked, poor little lady, but I pointed out that the rubber was bent backward and wasn't working, so she flushed the toilet without thinking and the brown water rose over the side and spilled to the floor. It went everywhere: shit water over to the closet where it began to soak the towels, and out the door into the bedroom. My mother screeched for Al.

"Al! Alllllllllll!"

I told her to please be quiet because I didn't want anyone in there; it was so goddamn embarrassing. All I had wanted to do was take a shit in peace and now it was all over the floor and she was alerting the whole gang. I told her to get me a bunch of towels and I would buy her new ones. She brought in an armful of old ragged ones. I was saddened by their condition but used them to mop the floor. It was so disgusting I almost puked.

I cursed more because I was so frustrated. I cursed about the shit, and about how my mother had stupidly flushed the toilet when I didn't even want her help, but I was also secretly cursing about the condition of the house. My mother overheard me and a minute later I could hear her down the hall, crying in Al's arms.

She was crying because of my cursing, because I sounded harsh, but she was also crying about the oven, and what it was really, truly about was seeing my father in the wedding film. And hell, I look like my father.

The toilet clogged and then was unclogged and all her pent-up emotion spilled over.

*

So, the year was finished by going to Yosemite and playing my father in a film adaptation of a story I wrote called "Yosemite," based on a trip I took as a kid with my father and brother. I designed that story so that it had references to the Old Testament, and even though it was simple on the surface, it was very deep otherwise, just like the Kelley Reichardt film *Old Joy*: people in nature, seemingly doing little but feeling everything.

I had played Mr. B in the other film based on my stories, and I now played my father. It was very strange because I started to see things from his side: all the trouble he must have gone through to take me and my brother up to Yosemite, requesting time off, paying for the Ahwahnee Hotel (not cheap), trying to get us to appreciate nature. And there we were, complaining the whole time.

On the particular trip I wrote about, we came across a few strange things: In some caves there were candles arranged in ritual shapes. Then, when we were walking back to the hotel, as the sun was setting, there were huge burning piles of leaves by the road. Near one of these piles we saw the ribcage of a skeleton. It was so scary. We were so young. My father told us that it was probably a mountain climber who had fallen off the mountain, and his body had been eaten by animals.

When we got back to the Ahwahnee it was late and all was scary because the image of the skeleton haunted us. My father called the park rangers and they told him that it had been a bear skeleton—that they had shot the bear because it had been getting too close to humans, because it was used to getting food from them. That night I had believed my father and his story about what the rangers told him, but when I put everything in the story, readers thought the father character was lying about the bear. So strange how stories make people see things differently. Like when people in my writing workshops thought my teenage boy characters were Columbine types, capable of killing, just because they had feelings.

I played my dad in *Yosemite*, and I felt for him. We eerily shot at all the actual places he had taken us: Mirror Lake, Yosemite Falls, the base of El Capitan, and of course the Ahwahnee Hotel, the place that was partial inspiration for the hotel in *The Shining*. The kids who played the young versions of my brother and me were sweet, but I could see how unaware they were of the gift my father had given us. I suppose that was something only my siblings and I could know, in our own little worlds.

And, in the end, the experiences have lasted, because here I am still thinking about them, writing about them, and acting them out.

Here's a little poem to finish this thing off:

WHEN I HIT THIRTY-FOUR

I looked around for love
And I knew by then
That love wasn't worship,
That love was ease.

Love was the smooth river
Of forgiveness that takes all
Obstacles, pollution, and debris
(Love is of man, he sets the rules),

Pushes them downstream,
And leaves them in the ocean.
I like the beer bottles that collect
Along the shore, the trash

From diaper boxes, and Clorox.
These are the rainbow-colored
Punctuations stuck into nature,
They are the man-made things

Corroded by my love.
I assume things will pile
And pile until the piles
Take over. But sometimes

Things are washed clean,
Like when a hurricane comes
Through and takes out houses
As if they were cardboard.

Love is not of man,
Nature sets the rules.
I've lived a life,
I've learned a few things

And this is a new lesson,
                    It says,

INSIGHT EDITIONS

PO Box 3088
San Rafael, CA 94912
www.insighteditions.com

Library of Congress Cataloging-in-Publication Data available.

ISBN: 978-1-60887-343-2

Publisher: Raoul Goff
Acquisitions Manager: Robbie Schmidt
Executive Editor: Vanessa Lopez
Editor: Talia Platz
Art Director: Chrissy Kwasnik
Book Designer: Nicole Poor
Production Manager: Jane Chinn

 Find us on Facebook: www.facebook.com/InsightEditions
 Follow us on Twitter: @insighteditions

ROOTS of PEACE   REPLANTED PAPER

Insight Editions, in association with Roots of Peace, will plant two trees for each tree used in
the manufacturing of this book. Roots of Peace is an internationally renowned humanitarian
organization dedicated to eradicating land mines worldwide and converting war-torn lands
into productive farms and wildlife habitats. Roots of Peace will plant two million fruit and nut
trees in Afghanistan and provide farmers there with the skills and support necessary for
sustainable land use.

Manufactured in China by Insight Editions

10 9 8 7 6 5 4 3 2 1